SNOW
IN
APRIL

SNOW IN APRIL

ROSAMUNDE PILCHER

St. Martin's Press

SNOW
IN
APRIL

Banked in scented steam, with her hair wound up in a bathcap, Caroline Cliburn lay supine in the bath and listened to the radio. The bathroom was large—as all the rooms in this generous house were large. It had once been a dressing-room, but long ago Diana had decided that people neither used nor needed dressing-rooms any longer, and she had stripped it naked, and called in plumbers and carpenters, and fitted it out with pink porcelain and a thick white carpet and hung floor-length chintz curtains at the window. There was a low glass-topped table, for bath salts and magazines and large eggs of pink soap, smelling of roses. There were roses, too, on the French bath-towels and the bath-mat, on which now reposed Caroline's dressing-gown, her slippers, the radio and a book which she had started to read and then abandoned.

The radio played a waltz. One-two-three, one-two-three went the sighing violins, conjuring up visions of palm courts and gentlemen in white gloves, and elderly ladies sitting on gilt chairs and nodding their heads in time to the pretty tune.

She thought, *I'll wear the new trouser suit.* And then remembered that one of the gilt buttons had fallen off the jacket and was now, in all probability, lost. It would, of course, be perfectly possible to look for the button, to thread a needle, to sew it on. The operation would take no more than five minutes, but it would be far simpler not to. To wear

1

instead the turquoise caftan, or the black velvet midi dress that Hugh said made her look like Alice in Wonderland.

The water was growing cold. She turned on the hot tap with her toe and told herself that at half past seven she would get out of the bath, get dried, put on a face and go downstairs. She would be late, but it wouldn't matter. They would all be waiting for her, grouped around the fireplace, Hugh in the velvet dinner jacket that she secretly disliked and Shaun girthed in his scarlet cummerbund. And the Haldanes would be there, Elaine well into her second Martini, and Parker with his knowing, suggestive eyes, and the guests of honour, Shaun's business associates from Canada, Mr and Mrs Grimandull, or some such name. And, after a reasonable delay, they would all troop in to dinner, turtle soup and the cassoulet Diana had spent the morning concocting, and a sensational pudding which would probably be brought in flaming, to the accompaniment of oohs and aahs and "Darling Diana, how do you do it?"

The thought of all that food made her feel, as usual, nauseated. It was puzzling. Indigestion was surely the prerogative of the very old, the greedy, or possibly, the pregnant, and Caroline, at twenty, could qualify for none of these. She didn't exactly feel ill, she just never felt well. Perhaps before next Tuesday—no, next Tuesday week—she should go to a doctor. She imagined trying to explain. *I'm going to be married and I feel sick all the time.* She saw his smile, paternal and understanding. *Pre-wedding nerves, natural enough, I'll give you a sedative . . .*

The waltz faded discreetly out, and the announcer came in with the seven-thirty news bulletin. Caroline sighed and sat up, pulled out the plug before she could succumb to the temptation of further basking, and climbed out on to the bath-mat. She turned off the radio, dried herself in a cursory fashion, pulled on the dressing-gown and padded through to her bedroom, leaving wet footmarks on the pale white carpet. She sat at her skirted dressing-table, pulled off the bathcap, and observed, without enthusiasm, her triply-reflected image. Her hair was long and straight and pale as milk, and hung, on either side of her face, like two silk tassels. It was not a pretty face in the accepted sense of the word. The cheekbones were too high, the nose blunt, the mouth wide. She knew that she could look either hideous or beautiful, and only her eyes, wide-set, dark brown and thickly-lashed, were consistently remarkable, even now when she was plain with tiredness.

(She remembered Drennan, and something he had once said, long ago, holding her head between his hands and turning her face up to his. "How is it that you have a boy's grin and a woman's eyes? And the eyes of a woman in love, at that?" They had been sitting in the front of his car, and outside it had been very dark and raining. She remembered the sound of the rain, the ticking of the car clock, the feel of his hands encircling her chin, but it was like remembering an incident in a book or a film, an incident that she had witnessed, but taken no part in. It had happened to another girl.)

She reached, abruptly, for her brush, disposed of her hair in a twist of rubber band, and began to make up her face. While she was in the middle of this, footsteps came down the passage, soft on the thick carpet, and stopped at her door. The door was lightly tapped.

"Hallo?"

"Can I come in?" It was Diana.

"Of course."

Her stepmother was already dressed in white and gold, her grey-blonde hair wound like a shell, speared with a gold pin. She looked, as always, beautiful, slender, tall, immaculately groomed. Her eyes were blue, accentuated by a tan which was maintained by regular sessions with a sunlamp, and one of the reasons why she was so often mistaken for a Scandinavian. And indeed, she possessed that happy ability to look as good in casual ski-clothes or tweeds as she did now, dressed and ready for an evening of the utmost formality.

"Caroline, you aren't nearly ready!"

Caroline began to do complicated things with her eye-lash brush.

"I'm half-way there. You know how quick I can be once I start." She added, "It's perhaps the only thing I learned at Drama School that's going to be of lasting use to me. You know, putting on a face in one minute flat."

This was a remark thoughtlessly made and instantly regretted. Drama School was still forbidden territory as far as Diana was concerned and her hackles went up at the very mention of the words. She said coolly, "In that case, perhaps the two years you spent there weren't entirely wasted," and when Caroline, crushed, made no reply, she went on, "Anyway, there's no hurry. Hugh's here, Shaun's giving him a drink now, but the Lundstroms will be a little late. She telephoned from the Connaught to say that John has been held up at a conference."

"Lundstrom. I couldn't remember their name. I've been calling them the Grimandulls."

"That's very unfair. You've not even met them."

"Have you?"

"Yes, and they're very nice."

She began, in a pointed fashion, to tidy up after Caroline, moving about her bedroom, pairing shoes, folding a sweater, gathering up the damp bath-towel which lay in the middle of the floor. This she folded and carried back to the bathroom, where Caroline could hear her making efforts to clean the basin, opening and shutting the door of the mirrored cupboard, doubtless putting back the lid on a jar of cold cream.

She raised her voice. "Diana, what does Mr Lundstrom confer about?"

"Um?" Diana re-appeared and Caroline repeated her question. "He's a banker."

"Is he involved in this new deal of Shaun's?"

"Very much so. He's backing it. That's why he's in this country, to get the last few details finalized."

"So, we'll all have to be very charming and well-behaved."

Caroline stood up, dropped off her dressing-gown and went naked, in search of clothes.

Diana sat on the end of the bed. "Is that such an effort? Caroline, you're dreadfully thin. Really too thin, you ought to try and put on a little weight."

"I'm all right." She picked some underclothes out of an overflowing drawer and began to put them on. "Just made this way."

"Rubbish. All your ribs are showing. And you don't eat enough to keep a fly alive. Even Shaun noticed the other day and you know how unobservant he usually is." Caroline pulled on a pair of tights. "And your colour's so bad, so pale. I noticed it just now when I came in. Perhaps you should start taking iron."

"Doesn't that turn your teeth black?"

"Now, where did you hear that old wives' tale?"

"Perhaps it's something to do with getting married. Having to write one hundred and forty-three thank you letters."

"Don't be ungrateful . . . oh, incidentally, Rose Kintyre was on the telephone, wondering what you wanted for a present. I suggested

4

those goblets you saw in Sloane Street, you know, the ones with the engraved initials. What are you going to wear this evening?"

Caroline opened her wardrobe and took down the first dress which came to hand, which happened to be the black velvet. "This?"

"Yes. I love that dress. But you should wear dark stockings with it."

Caroline put it back, took out the next. "Then this?" The caftan, luckily not the trouser suit.

"Yes. Charming. With gold ear-rings."

"I've lost mine."

"Oh, *not* the ones that Hugh gave you."

"Not really lost, just mislaid. I've put them somewhere but I can't remember where. Don't bother." She tossed the turquoise silk, soft as thistledown over her head. "Earrings don't show on me, anyway, unless my hair's been properly done." She began to do up the tiny buttons. She said, "What about Jody? Where's he having dinner?"

"With Katy, in the basement, I said he could have it with us, but he wants to watch the Western on television."

Caroline loosened her hair and brushed it smooth. "Is he there now?"

"I think so."

Caroline sprayed herself at random with the first bottle of scent that came to hand. "If you don't mind," she said, "I'll go down first and say good night to him."

"Don't be too long. The Lundstroms will be here in about ten minutes."

"I won't."

They went downstairs together. As they descended into the hall the door of the drawing-room opened and Shaun Carpenter emerged, carrying a red ice-jar which was shaped like an apple and had a gilt stalk sticking up from its lid to form a handle. He looked up and saw them.

"No ice," he said by way of explanation and then was diverted, like a stage comedian doing a double-take, by their appearance, and stood still, in the middle of the hall, to witness their descent.

"Well, don't you both look beautiful? What a pair of gorgeous women."

Shaun was Diana's husband, and Caroline's . . . her mode of

reference varied. My stepmother's husband she sometimes called him. Or, my step-step-father. Or, simply, Shaun.

He and Diana had been married for three years, but, as he was fond of telling people, he had known her and adored her for far longer than that.

"Knew her in the old days," he would say. "Thought I had the whole business neatly buttoned up, and then she went off to the Greek Islands to buy a piece of property, and the next thing I new, she was writing to tell me she'd met and got herself married off to this architect fellow—Gerald Cliburn. Not a bean to his name, a ready-made family and as Bohemian as hell. You could have knocked me down with a feather."

He had remained faithful to her memory, however, and being a naturally successful man, had made an equal success of his role as professional bachelor, the older, more sophisticated man, much in demand by London hostesses and never without a diary packed with engagements for months to come.

Indeed, his single life was so remarkably well-organized and pleasant that when Diana Cliburn, widowed and with two stepchildren in tow, returned to London to move back into her old house, pick up the old threads and start life anew, there was certain speculation about what Shaun Carpenter would do now. Had he dug himself to deeply into his comfortable bachelor rut? Would he—even for Diana —give up his independence and settle for the humdrum life of an ordinary family man? Gossip doubted it very much.

But gossip had reckoned without Diana. She returned from Aphros if anything more beautiful and desirable than ever. She was now thirty-two and at the height of her attraction. Shaun, cautiously renewing their friendship, was bowled over in a matter of days. Within a week he had asked her to marry him and repeated himself at regular seven-day intervals until she finally agreed.

The first thing she made him do was to break the news, himself, to Caroline and Jody. "I can't be a father," he had told them, pacing the drawing-room carpet and going warm round the collar beneath their clear and oddly identical gazes. "Wouldn't know how to, anyway. But I'd like you to feel that you can always make use of me, as a confidant or possible financier . . . after all, this is your home . . . and I'd like you to feel . . ."

He floundered on, cursing Diana for having put him in this awkward situation and wishing that she had let well alone and allowed his relationship with Caroline and Jody to develop slowly and naturally. But Diana was impatient by nature, she liked everything cut and dried and she liked it cut and dried now.

Jody and Caroline watched Shaun, sympathetic, but saying and doing nothing to help him out. They liked Shaun Carpenter, but saw, with the clear eyes of youth, that already Diana had him in the palm of her hand. And he spoke about Milton Gardens as their home, whereas home, to them, was and always would be, a white cube like sugar loaf, perched high above the navy-blue Aegean Sea. But that was gone, sunk without trace into the confusion of the past. What Diana chose to do, whom she chose now to marry, could be none of their business. However, if she had to marry anyone, they were glad it was the large and kindly Shaun.

Now, as Caroline moved to go past him, he stood aside, courtly and starched and faintly ridiculous with the ice bucket held like an offering in his hands. He smelt of "Brut" and the clean smell of fresh linen, and Caroline remembered her father's frequently stubbly chin and the blue work-shirts that he preferred to wear straight from the washing line without so much as a touch of an iron. She remembered, too, the fights and arguments that he and Diana had cheerfully indulged in and which her father almost always won! and she was newly amazed that one woman could find it possible to marry two men who were so remotely different.

Descending to the basement and Katy's domain was like going from one world to another. Upstairs were the pastel carpets, the chandeliers, the heavy velvet curtains. Downstairs, all was cluttered, uncontrived and cheerful. Checked linoleum vied with vivid rugs, curtains were patterned with zig-zags and leaves, every horizontal surface bore its burden of photographs, china ash-trays from forgotten seaside resorts, painted shells and vases of plastic flowers. A proper fire burned redly in the fireplace and in front of it, curled up in a sagging armchair and with his eyes glued to the quivering television screen, was Caroline's brother Jody.

He wore jeans and a navy polo-necked sweater, battered chukka boots, and for no particular reason, a ramshackle yachting cap, several sizes too large for him. He looked up as she came in, and then went immediately back to the screen. He didn't want to miss a single shot, a single second of the action.

Caroline edged him over in the chair and let herself down beside him. After a little she said, "Who's the girl?"

"Oh, she's stupid. She's always kissing. It's one of those."

"Turn it off then."

He considered this, decided that perhaps it was a good idea; and climbed out of the chair to turn off the set. The television died with a small moan. He stood on the hearthrug, looking down at her.

He was eleven, a good age, out of babyhood, but not yet tall and scrawny and bad-tempered and troubled by spots. His features were so like Caroline's own that strangers, seeing them for the first time, knew that they could be nothing but brother and sister, but while Caroline was fair, Jody had hair of so bright a brown that it verged on red, and while her freckles confined themselves to a smattering across the bridge of her nose, Jody's were all over, scattered like confetti across his back and his shoulders and down his arms. His eyes were grey. His smile, which was slow, but disarming when it did appear, revealed second teeth too big for his face and a little crooked, as though they jostled to make space for themselves.

"Where's Katy?" Caroline asked.

"Upstairs in the kitchen."

"Have you had dinner?"

"Yes."

"Did you get what we're having?"

"I had some soup. But I didn't want the other thing so Katy cooked bacon and eggs."

"I wish I could have had it with you. Did you see Shaun and Hugh?"

"Yes. I went up." He made a face. "The Haldanes are coming, bad luck on you."

They smiled in conspiracy. Their views on the Haldanes had a certain sameness. Caroline said, "Where'd you get the hat?"

He had forgotten about the hat. Now he took it off, looking bashful. "I just found it. In the old dressing-up box in the nursery."

"It was Poppa's."

"Yes. I thought it probably was."

Caroline leaned over and took it from him. The hat was dirty and bent, stained with salt, the badge beginning to come loose from its stitches. "He used to wear it when he went sailing. He used to say that being properly dressed gave him confidence so that when someone swore at him for doing the wrong thing, he just used to swear right back." Jody grinned. "Do you remember him saying things like that?"

"Some," said Jody. "I remember him reading Rikki Tikki Tavi."

"You were just a little boy. Six years old. But you remember that." He smiled again. Caroline got up and put the old hat back on his head. The peak obliterated his face so that she had to stoop to reach beneath it to kiss him.

"Good night," she said.

"Good night," said Jody, not moving.

She was reluctant to leave him. At the foot of the stairs she turned back. He was watching her intently from beneath the peak of the ridiculous cap and there was something in his eyes that made her say, "What's wrong?"

"Nothing."

"I'll see you tomorrow then."

"Yes," said Jody. "Sure. Good night."

Upstairs again she found the drawing-room door shut, a hum of voices coming from beyond, and Katy putting a dark fur coat on to a hanger and disposing of it in the cupboard by the front door. Katy wore her maroon dress and a flowered apron, her concession to the formality of a dinner party, and she started dramatically when Caroline suddenly appeared.

"Ooh, you didn't arf give me a start."

"Who's come?"

"Mr and Mrs Aldane." She jerked her head. "They're in there now. You'd better get a move on, you're late."

"I just saw Jody." Reluctant to join the party, she stayed with Katy, leaning against the bottom on the banister. She imagined the bliss of going back upstairs, climbing into bed, being brought a boiled egg.

"Still watching those Indians?"

"I don't think so. He said there was too much kissing."

Katy made a face. "Better watch kissing than all that violence, that's what I say." She shut the cupboard door. "I'd rather have them wondering what it's all about, than going out and coshing old ladies with their own umbrellas."

And with this telling observation she went back to her kitchen. Caroline, left alone and with no further excuse for delay, crossed the hall, put a smile on her face and opened the drawing-room door. (Another thing that she had learned at Drama School was how to make an entrance.) The buzz of chatter ceased and somebody said, "Here's Caroline."

Diana's drawing-room, at night, lit for a party, was as spectacular as any stage set. The three long windows which faced out over the quiet square were draped in pale, almond-green velvet. There were huge, squashy sofas in pink and beige, a beige carpet, and, blending marvellously with the old pictures, walnut cabinets and Chippendale, a modern coffee table, Italian in steel and glass. There were flowers everywhere and the air was pervaded with a variety of delicious and expensive smells; hyacinths and "Madame Rochas" and Shaun's Havana cigars.

They stood, just as she had imagined them, grouped around the fireplace, with drinks in their hands. But before she had even closed the door behind her, Hugh had detached himself from the group, laid down his glass and come across the room to meet her.

"Darling." He took her shoulders between his hands and bent to kiss her. Then he glanced at his wafer-thin gold wrist-watch, displaying as he did so an expanse of starched white cuff caught with links of knotted gold. "You're late."

"But the Lundstroms haven't even come yet."

"Where've you been?"

"With Jody."

"Then you're forgiven."

He was tall, much taller than Caroline, slim, swarthy, beginning to go bald. This made him look older than his actual age, which was thirty-three. He wore the midnight blue velvet dinner jacket and an evening shirt lightly touched with bands of embroidered lace, and his eyes, beneath the strongly marked brows, were a very dark brown and held, at this moment, an expression which contained amusement, exasperation, and a certain amount of pride.

Caroline saw the pride and was relieved. Hugh Rashley took a certain amount of living up to and Caroline spent half her time struggling with sensations of gross inadequacy. Otherwise he was, as a future husband, eminently satisfactory, successful in his chosen career of stockbroking and marvellously thoughtful and considerate even if his standards did sometimes reach unnecessary heights. But this, perhaps, was only to be expected, for it was a characteristic which ran in his family, and he was, after all, Diana's brother.

Because Parker Haldane was unrepentantly attracted to pretty young women and Caroline was one of them, Elaine Haldane's manner towards Caroline was habitually cool. This did not worry Caroline unduly; for one thing, she seldom met Elaine, for the Haldanes lived in Paris, where Parker was in charge of the French department of a big American advertising agency, and only came to London for important meetings, every two or three months. This visit was just such an occasion.

For another, she did not particularly like Elaine, which was unfortunate, for Elaine and Diana were the best of friends. "Why do you always have to be so off-hand with Elaine?" Diana would demand and Caroline had learned to shrug and say "I'm sorry," for any more detailed explanations could only cause the greatest offence.

Elaine was a handsome, distinguished woman, with a tendency to over-dress which even living in Paris had done nothing to cure. She could also be extremely amusing, but Caroline had learned, through bitter experience, that, buried in her witticisms were sharp barbs of verbal cruelty, directed at friends and acquaintances who did not happen, at the time, to be present. It was daunting to listen to her, because you could never be sure what she was planning to say about you.

Parker, on the other hand, was not to be taken seriously.

"You beautiful creature." He stooped to sketch a continental kiss over the back of Caroline's hand. She half expected him to click his heels. "Why do you always have to keep us waiting?"

"I was saying good night to Jody." She turned to his wife. "Good evening, Elaine." They touched cheeks, making kissing sounds in the air.

"Hallo, dear. What a pretty dress!"

"Thank you."

"They're so easy to wear, those loose things . . ." She took a pull at her cigarette, exhaled a huge cloud of smoke. "I've just been telling Diana about Elizabeth."

Caroline's heart sank, but she said, politely, "What about Elizabeth?" waiting to be told that Elizabeth was engaged; that Elizabeth had been staying with the Aga Khan; that Elizabeth was in New York, modelling for *Vogue*. Elizabeth was Elaine's daughter, by a previous marriage, and a little older than Caroline, but, despite the fact that Caroline sometimes felt she knew more about Elizabeth than she did about herself, they had never met. Elizabeth divided her time between her parents—mother in Paris and father in Scotland—and on the rare occasions when she turned up in London, Caroline was invariably away.

Now she tried to remember the latest news on Elizabeth. "Hasn't she been in the West Indies, or something?"

"Yes, my dear, staying with an old schoolfriend, having the most wonderful time. But she flew home a couple of days ago and was met at Prestwick by her father with this ghastly news."

"What news?"

"Well, you know, ten years ago, when Duncan and I were still together, we bought this place in Scotland . . . at least Duncan bought it, in the face of violent opposition from me . . . Marriage-wise, it was just the last straw." She stopped, a confused expression on her face.

"Elizabeth," Caroline prompted gently.

"Oh, of course. Well, the first thing Elizabeth did was to make friends with the two boys who lived on the neighbouring estate . . . well, not boys exactly, they were already grown-up when we first met them, but completely charming, and they just took Elizabeth under their wing like a little sister. Before you could snap your fingers she was in and out of their house as though she'd lived there all her life. They adored her, but she was always the special pet of the older brother, and my dear, just before she came home, he killed himself in the most terrible car smash. Too ghastly, icy roads, the car went straight into a stone wall."

Despite herself, Caroline was truly shocked. "Oh, how awful!"

"Oh, ghastly. Only twenty-eight. A wonderful farmer, marvellous shot, such a darling person. You can imagine what sort of a homecoming the poor darling had, she rang me up in tears to tell me, and I longed to get her to London and meet us here, and let us cheer her up, but she says she's needed up there . . ."

"I'm sure her father will love having her . . ." Parker chose this moment to materialize at Caroline's elbow, and handed her a Martini so cold that it nearly froze her fingers. He said, "Who are we waiting for?"

"The Lundstroms. They're Canadians. He's a banker from Montreal. It's all to do with this new project of Shaun's."

"Does that really mean that Diana and Shaun are going out to Montreal to live?" asked Elaine. "But what are we going to do without them? Diana, what are we going to do without you?"

Parker said, "How long are they going to be away?"

"Three, four years. Less perhaps. They leave as soon after the wedding as they can."

"And this house? Are you and Hugh going to live here?"

"It's much too big. Anyway, Hugh's got a perfectly adequate flat of his own. No, Katy's going to stay in the basement as a sort of caretaker, and Diana thought that she might let it if she could find the right sort of tenant."

"And Jody?"

Caroline looked at him, and then down at her drink.

"Jody's going with them. To live."

"Won't you mind that?"

"Yes, I'll mind. But Diana wants to take him."

And Hugh doesn't want to be saddled with a little boy. Not just yet, at any rate. A baby, perhaps, in a couple of years, but not a little boy of eleven. And Diana's already got him into a private school and Shaun says he'll have him taught how to ski and play ice hockey.

Parker was still watching her. She smiled wryly. "You know Diana, Parker. She makes plans, and bang, they happen."

"You'll miss him, won't you?"

"Yes, I'll miss him."

The Lundstroms arrived at last, were introduced, given drinks and drawn, politely, into the conversation. Caroline, moving aside on the pretence of finding a cigarette, watched them curiously and thought that they looked alike, as married people so often do, both tall and angular, rather sporty. She imagined them playing golf together at the week-ends or sailing—perhaps ocean racing—in the summer. Mrs Lundstrom's dress was simple, her diamonds sensational, and Mr Lundstrom had that certain colourless nonentity that often blurs the outline of a spectacularly successful man.

She thought, quite suddenly, that it would be wonderful, like a breath of fresh air, for someone to come into this house who was poor, a failure, without morals, or even drunk. An artist, perhaps, starving in a garret. An author who wrote stories that no one would buy. Or some cheerful beachcomber with a three-day growth of beard and an inelegant belly bulging over the belt of his trousers. She thought of her father's friends, ill-assorted and usually disreputable, drinking red wine or retsina well into the night, sleeping where they found themselves, on the sagging sofa, or with their feet propped on the low wall of the terrace. And she thought of the house on Aphros, at night, painted by moonlight in blocks of black and white, and always the sound of the sea.

". . . we're going in for dinner."

It was Hugh. She realized that he had already told her this and been forced to repeat himself. "You're dreaming, Caroline. Finish your drink, it's time to go and have something to eat."

At the dinner table, she found herself between John Lundstrom and Shaun. Shaun was busy with the wine decanter, and so she fell naturally into conversation with Mr Lundstrom.

"Is this your first visit to England?"

"Oh, by no means. I've been here many times before." He straightened his knife and fork, frowning slightly. "Now, I haven't got this quite straight. This family relationship, I mean. You're Diana's stepdaughter?"

"Yes, that's right. And I'm going to marry Hugh, who is her brother. Most people seem to think it's practically illegal, but it isn't really. I mean, there's nothing about it in the back of the prayer-book."

"I never thought for a moment that it was illegal. Simply very tidy. It keeps all the right people in the same family."

"Isn't that a little narrow minded?"

He looked up and smiled. He looked younger, gayer, and less rich when he smiled. More human. Caroline warmed to him.

"You could call it practical. When are you going to be married?"

"On Tuesday week. I can hardly believe it."

"And will you both come out to visit Shaun and Diana in Montreal?"

"I expect we shall later on. Not just yet."

"And then there's the little boy . . ."

"Yes. Jody, my brother."

"He's coming with them."

"Yes."

"He'll take to Canada like a duck to water. It's a great place for a boy."

"Yes," said Caroline again.

"There are just the two of you?"

"Oh, no," said Caroline. "There's Angus."

"Another brother?"

"Yes. He's nearly twenty-five."

"And what does he do?"

"We don't know."

John Lundstrom raised polite but surprised eyebrows. Caroline said, "I mean that. We don't know what he does and we don't know where he is. You see, we used to live on Aphros in the Aegean. My father was an architect, a sort of agent for people who wanted to buy property and build out there. That was how he met Diana."

"Now hold it. You mean, Diana came out to buy some land?"

"Yes, and build a house. But she didn't do either. She met my father and married him instead and she stayed out in Aphros with us all and lived in this house we'd always had . . ."

"But you came back to London?"

"Yes, my father died, you see, so Diana brought us back with her. But Angus said he wasn't coming. He was nineteen then, with hair down to his shoulders and not a pair of shoes to his name. And Diana said that if he wanted to stay in Aphros he could, but he said she might as well sell the house, because he'd acquired a secondhand Mini Moke and he was going to drive to India through Afghanistan. And Diana asked him what he was going to do when he got there, and Angus said, find himself."

"He's just one of thousands. You know that, don't you?"

"It doesn't make it any easier when he's your brother."

"Haven't you seen him since?"

"Yes. He came back soon after Diana and Shaun were married, but you know how these things go. We all thought he'd at least have a pair of shoes on his feet, but he was unchanged and unrepentant and everything Diana suggested just made him worse, so he went back to Afghanistan again, and we haven't heard from him since."

"Not at all?"

"Well . . . once. A picture postcard of Kabul or Srinagar or Tehran or somewhere." She smiled, trying to make a joke of it, but before John Lundstrom could think up any sort of a reply, Katy leaned over his shoulder to set down a bowl of turtle soup, and, with the conversation broken, he turned away from Caroline and started instead to talk to Elaine.

The evening wore on, formal, predictable and, to Caroline, boring. After coffee and brandy they all foregathered once more in the drawing-room. The men gravitated into one corner to talk business, the women gathered by the fire, gossiped, made plans for Canada, admired the tapestry on which Diana was currently working.

After a little, Hugh detached himself from the group of men, ostensibly to refill John Lundstrom's glass. But when he had done this, he came over to Caroline's side, sat on the arm of her chair and said, "How are you?"

"Why do you ask?"

"Are you well enough to go to Arabella's?"

She looked up at him. From the depth of the armchair his face appeared almost upside down. It looked odd.

"What time is it?" she asked.

He glanced at his watch. "Eleven. Perhaps you're too tired?"

Before she could reply, Diana, overhearing the conversation, looked up from her tapestry and said, "Off you go, the two of you."

"Where are they off to?" asked Elaine.

"Arabella's. It's a little club Hugh belongs to . . ."

"Sounds intriguing . . ." Elaine smiled at Hugh, looking as though she knew all about intriguing night clubs. Hugh and Caroline excused themselves, said good night to the company and left. Caroline went upstairs to fetch a coat, paused to comb her hair. At Jody's door she stopped, but the light was off and no sound came from within, so she decided not to disturb him, and went downstairs again to where Hugh waited for her in the hall. He opened the door for her and they went out together into the soft, windy darkness, and walked down the pavement to where he had parked his car, and drove around the Square and out into Kensington High Street, and she saw that there was the beginnings of a moon, and rags of cloud were being driven across its face by the wind. The trees in the park tossed their bare branches; the orange glow of the city was reflected in the sky, and Caroline rolled down the window and let the cool air blow her hair and thought that on such a night, one should be in the country, walking along dark, unlighted roads, with the wind soughing in the trees and only the fitful moonlight to show the way.

She sighed. "What's that for?" asked Hugh.

"What's what for?"

"The sigh. It sounded like tragedy."

"It's nothing."

After a little, "Everything's all right?" Hugh asked. "You're not worried about anything?"

"No." There was, after all nothing to be worried about. Nothing, and everything. Feeling ill all the time was one of them. She wondered why it was impossible to talk to Hugh about this. Perhaps because he was always so fit himself. Energetic, active, full of energy and apparently never tired. At any rate, it was boring to be in ill-health, doubly boring to talk about it.

The silence between them grew. At last, waiting for traffic lights to change from red to green, Hugh said, "The Lundstroms are delightful."

"Yes. I told Mr Lundstrom about Angus and he listened."

"What else did you expect him to do?"

"Just what everybody else always does. Look shocked and horrified and delighted—or change the subject. Diana hates us to talk about Angus. I suppose because he was her one failure." She corrected herself. "*Is* her one failure."

"You mean because he didn't come back to London with you all."

"Yes, and learn how to be a chartered accountant or whatever career it was she had planned for him. Instead, he did exactly what he wanted to do."

"At the risk of being told that I am taking Diana's part in this argument, I would say, so did you. In the teeth of all opposition you got yourself to Drama School and even managed to hold down a job . . ."

"For six months. That was all."

"You were ill. You had pneumonia. That wasn't your fault."

"No. But I got better and if I'd been worth my salt, I'd have gone back and tried again. But I didn't, I chickened out. And Diana had always said that I hadn't got the staying power, so in the end, inevitably, she was right. The only thing she didn't say was 'I told you so.' "

"But if you'd still been on the stage," said Hugh gently, "you probably wouldn't be getting married to me."

Caroline glanced at his profile, strangely lit by overhead street lights and the glow from the dashboard. He looked saturnine, slightly villainous.

"No. I don't suppose I would."

But it wasn't as simple as that. The reasons she had for marrying Hugh were legion and so bound up with each other that it was hard to disentangle them. But gratitude seemed the most important. Hugh had come into her life when she had returned from Aphros with Diana, a stringy fifteen-year-old. But even then, sullen and inarticulate with unhappiness, watching Hugh cope with luggage and passports and a tired and weeping Jody, she had recognized his qualities. He was just the sort of reliable male relation she had always needed but never known. And it was pleasant to be ordered about and taken care of, and his protective attitude—not paternal, exactly, but certainly avuncular—had endured through the difficult years of growing up.

Another force to be reckoned with was Diana herself. From the very beginning, she seemed to have decided that Hugh and Caroline were the perfect match. The very orderliness of the arrangement appealed to her. Subtly, for she was too clever to indulge in any obvious action, she encouraged them to be together. *Hugh can drive you to the station. Darling, will you be in for dinner, Hugh's coming and I want you to make up the numbers.*

But even this relentless pressure would have been of no avail if it had not been for the affair that Caroline had with Drennan Colefield. After that . . . after loving that way, it seemed to Caroline that nothing could ever be quite the same again. When it was all over, and she could look around without her eyes filling with tears, she saw that Hugh was still there. Waiting for her. Unchanged—except that now he wanted to marry her, and now there seemed no reason on earth why she shouldn't.

He said, "You've been quiet all evening."

"I thought I was talking too much."

"You'd tell me if anything was worrying you?"

"Only that things are happening too quickly, and there's so much to do, and meeting the Lundstroms makes me feel as though Jody's already gone to Canada and I'm never going to see him again."

Hugh fell silent, reaching for a cigarette, and lighting it from the gadget on the dashboard. He replaced the lighter, and said, "I'm fairly

certain that what you're suffering from is Bridal Depression or whatever it is the Women's Page always calls it."

"Caused by what?"

"Too many things to think about; too many letters to write; too
many presents to unpack. Clothes to try on, curtains to choose, caterers and florists beating at the door. It's enough to drive the sanest girl
off her nut."

"Then why did you let us be railroaded into this huge wedding?"

"Because we both mean a lot to Diana, and to have slunk off to a
Registry Office and then spent two days at Brighton would have done
her out of endless pleasure."

"But we're people, not sacrificial lambs."

He put a hand over hers. "Cheer up. It'll soon be Tuesday and
then it'll be over and we'll be flying to the Bahamas and you can lie in
the sun all day and not write a single letter to anybody and eat nothing
but oranges. How does that appeal to you?"

She said, knowing she was being childish, "I wish we were going
to Aphros."

Hugh began to sound impatient. "Caroline, you know we've been
over this a thousand times . . ."

She stopped listening to him, her thoughts jerked back to Aphros
like a fish on a line. She remembered the olive orchards, ancient trees
knee-deep in poppies, against a back-drop of azure sea. And fields of
grape-hyacinths and pale scented pink cyclamen. And the sound of
bells from the herds of goats and the scent in the mountains, of pine,
running warm, dripping with resin.

". . . anyway, it's all been arranged."

"But, one day, shall we go to Aphros, Hugh?"

"You haven't been listening to a single word I've said."

"We could rent a little house."

"No."

"Or hire a yacht."

"No."

"Why don't you want to go?"

"Because I think you should remember it the way it was, not the
way it may be now, spoiled by developers and sky-scraper hotels."

"You don't know it's like that."

19

"I have a very shrewd idea."

"But . . ."

"No," said Hugh.

After a pause, she said, stubbornly, "I still want to go back."

2

The clock in the hall was striking two when they at last got home. The chimes rang out, stately and mellow, as Hugh put Caroline's key into the lock and pushed open the black door. Inside, the hall light burned, but the staircase rose to darkness. It was very quiet, the party was long since over and everybody had gone to bed.

She turned to Hugh. "Good night."

"Good night, darling." They kissed. "When shall I see you again? I'm out of town tomorrow evening . . . perhaps Tuesday?"

"Come round for dinner. I'll tell Diana."

"You do that."

He smiled, went out, began to close the door. She remembered to say "Thank you for the lovely evening" before the door clicked shut and then she was alone. She waited, listening for his car.

When the sound of the engine had died away, she turned and went upstairs a step at a time, holding the banister rail. At the top of the stairs, she turned off the hall light and went along the passage to her bedroom. The curtains were drawn, the bed turned down, her nightdress laid across the foot of the quilt. Shedding shoes, bag, coat and scarf in her progress across the carpet, she reached the bed at last and flopped across it, careless of any damage that she might do to her dress. After a little she put up a hand and began, slowly, to undo the tiny buttons, pulled the caftan over her head and then the rest of her

21

clothes; she put on her nightdress, and it felt cool and light against her skin. Barefoot, she padded through to the bathroom, washed her face in a cursory fashion and scrubbed her teeth. This refreshed her. She was still tired, but her brain was as active as a squirrel in its cage. She went back to her dressing table and picked up her brush, and then, deliberately, laid down the brush and opened the bottom drawer of the dressing-table and took out the letters from Drennan, the bundle still tied in red ribbon, and the photograph of them both, feeding the pigeons in Trafalgar Square; and the old theatre programmes and the menus and all the little worthless scraps of paper that she had collected and treasured simply because they were the only tangible way of pinning down the memories of the time they had spent together.

You were ill, Hugh had said this evening, making excuses for her. *You had pneumonia.*

It sounded so obvious, so straightforward. But none of them, not even Diana, had known about Drennan Colefield. Even when it was all over and Diana and Caroline were alone together in Antibes where Diana had taken her to convalesce, Caroline never told her what had really happened, although she longed sometimes for the comfort of old clichés. *Time is the great healer. Every girl has to have at least one unhappy love affair in her life. There's better fish in the sea than ever came out of it.*

Months later, his name had come up at breakfast. Diana was reading the paper, the theatre page, and she looked up and said to Caroline, across the sunlight and the marmalade and the smell of coffee, "Wasn't Drennan Colefield at Lunnbridge Repertory when you were down there?"

Caroline, very carefully, laid down her cup of coffee and said, "Yes. Why?"

"It says here he's going to play Kirby Ashton in the film of *Bring Out Your Gun*. I should think that would be a pretty meaty part, the book was all sex and violence and gorgeous girls." She looked up. "Was he good? I mean as an actor?"

"Yes, I suppose he was."

"There's a photo of him here with his wife. Did you know he'd married Michelle Tyler? He looks terribly handsome."

And she had handed the paper over, and there he was, thinner than Caroline remembered, and the hair longer, but still the smile, the light in the eye, the cigarette between his fingers.

"What are you doing tonight?" he had asked the first time they had ever met. She had been making coffee in the Green Room and was covered in paint from working on the scenery. And she had said "Nothing," and Drennan said "So am I. Let's do nothing together." And after that evening the world became an unbelievably beautiful place. Each leaf on every tree was suddenly a miracle. A child playing with a ball, an old man sitting on a park bench, were filled with a meaning that she had never recognized. The dull little town was transformed, the people who lived in it smiled and looked happy and the sun always seemed to be shining, warmer and brighter than ever before. And all this because of Drennan. *This is how it is to love,* he had told her and showed her. *This is how it is meant to be.*

But it was never like that again. Remembering Drennan and loving him; knowing that in a week she was going to marry Hugh, Caroline began to cry. There were no sobs or disturbing sounds, simply a flood of tears that filled her eyes and streamed down her cheeks, unchecked and unheeded.

She might have sat there till morning, staring at her reflection, wallowing in self-pity and coming to no worthwhile conclusion if she had not been disturbed by Jody. He came soundlessly down the passage which separated his room from hers and tapped at the door, and then, when she did not reply, opened the door and put his head round.

"Are you all right?" he asked.

His unexpected appearance was as good as a douche of cold water. Caroline at once made an effort to pull herself together, wiped at her tears with the flat of her hand, reached for a dressing-gown to pull over her nightdress.

"Yes . . . of course I am . . . what are you doing out of bed?"

"I was awake. I heard you come in. Then I heard you moving around and I thought you might be feeling sick." He closed the door behind him and came over to where she sat. He wore blue pyjamas and his feet were bare, and his red hair stuck up in a crest at the back.

"What were you crying about?"

It was useless to say "I wasn't crying." Caroline said "Nothing" which was just about as useless.

"You can't say 'nothing.' It isn't possible to cry about nothing." He came close, his eyes on a level with hers. "Are you hungry?"

She smiled, and shook her head.

"I am. I thought I'd go downstairs and find something."

"You do that."

But he stayed where he was, his eyes moving around, searching for clues as to what had made her unhappy. They fell on the bundle of letters, the photograph. He reached out and picked this up. "That's Drennan Colefield. I saw him in *Bring Out Your Gun.* I had to get Katy to take me because it was an A Certificate. He was Kirby Ashton. He was super." He looked up at Caroline. "You knew him, didn't you?"

"Yes. We were at Lunnbridge together."

"He's married now."

"I know."

"Is *that* why you were crying?"

"Perhaps."

"Did you know him as well as that?"

"Oh, Jody, it was all over a long time ago."

"Then why does it make you cry?"

"I'm just being sentimental."

"But you . . ." He stumbled over the use of the word "Love." "You're going to marry Hugh."

"I know. That's what being sentimental means. It means crying over something that's finished, over and done with. And it's a waste of time."

Jody stared at her intently. After a little, he laid down the photograph of Drennan and said, "I'm going down to find a piece of cake. I'll come back. Do you want anything?"

"No. Go quietly. Don't wake Diana."

He slipped away. Caroline put the letters and the photograph back into the drawer, closed it firmly. Then she went to collect the clothes she had discarded, hung up her caftan, treed her shoes, folded the other things and laid them over a chair. By the time Jody returned, bearing his snack on a tray, she had brushed her hair, and was sitting up in bed, waiting for him. He came to settle himself beside her, edging the tray on to her bedside table.

He said, "You know, I've got an idea."

"A good one?"

"I think so. You see, you think I don't mind going to Canada with Diana and Shaun. But I do. I don't want to go in the very least. I'd rather do anything than go."

Caroline stared at him. "But, Jody, I thought you wanted to go. You seemed so keen on the idea."

"I was being polite."

"For heaven's sake, you can't be polite when it's a question of going to Canada."

"I can. But now I'm telling you that I don't want to go."

"But Canada will be fun."

"How do you know it'll be fun? You've never been there. Besides I don't want to leave this school and my friends and the football team."

Caroline was mystified. "But why didn't you tell me this before? Why are you telling me now?"

"I didn't tell you *before* because you were always so busy with letters and toast-racks and veils and things."

"But never too busy for *you* . . ."

He went on as though she had never spoken. "And I'm telling you *now* because if I don't tell you now it'll be too late. There just won't be time. So do you want to hear about my plan?"

She was suddenly apprehensive. "I don't know. What is your plan?"

"I think I should stay here in London, and not go to Montreal . . . no, not stay with you and Hugh. With Angus."

"Angus?" It was almost funny. "Angus is in the back of beyond. Kashmir, or Nepal or somewhere. Even if we knew how to get hold of him, which we don't, he'd never come back to London."

"He's not in Kashmir, or Nepal," said Jody taking a large mouthful of cake. "He's in *Scotland.*"

His sister stared at him, wondering if she had heard aright through all the cake crumbs and sultanas. *"Scotland?"* He nodded. "What makes you think he's in *Scotland?*"

"I don't think. I know. He wrote me a letter. I got it about three weeks ago. He's working at the Strathcorrie Arms Hotel, Strathcorrie, Perthshire."

"He wrote you a letter? And you never told me?"

Jody's face closed up. "I thought it better not to."

"Where is the letter now?"

"In my room." He took another maddening bite of his cake.

"Will you show it to me?"

"All right."

He slipped off the bed and disappeared, to return carrying the letter in his hand. "Here," he said and gave it to her, and climbed back on to the bed, and reached for his milk. The envelope was a cheap, buff-coloured one, the address typewritten. "Very anonymous," said Caroline.

"I know. I found it one day when I came back from school and I thought it was someone trying to sell me something. It looks like that, doesn't it? You know, when you write away for things . . ."

She took the letter out of the envelope, a single sheet of airmail paper, which had obviously been much handled and many times read, and felt as if it were about to fall apart.

Strathcorrie Arms Hotel,
Strathcorrie,
Perthshire.

My dear Jody,

 This is one of those messages you burn before reading because it is so secret. So don't let Diana get her peepers on it, otherwise my life won't be worth living.

 I returned from India about two months ago, finished up here with a chap I met in Persia. He has now departed and I managed to get myself a job in the hotel as boot boy and filler of coal buckets and log baskets. The place is full of old people up for the fishing. When they aren't fishing they sit about in chairs looking as though they had been dead for six months.

 I was in London for a couple of days after my ship docked in. Would have come to see you and Caroline, but terrified that Diana would corral me, halter me (in starched collars), shoe me (in black leather) and groom me (cut my hair). Then it would only be a matter of time before I was broken to harness and a nice safe ride for a lady.

 Send C. my love. Tell her I am well and happy. Will let you know next move.

I miss you both.

Angus.

"Jody, why didn't you show me this before?"

"I thought perhaps you'd feel you had to show Hugh and then he would tell Diana."

She re-read the letter. "He doesn't know I'm getting married."

"No, I don't suppose he does."

"We can ring him up."

But Jody was against this. "There's no phone number. And anyway, someone would hear. And anyway, phoning's no good, you can't see the other person's face, and you always get cut off." She knew that he hated the telephone, was even frightened of it.

"Well, we could write him a letter."

"He never replies to letters."

This was too true. But Caroline was uneasy, Jody was driving at something and she didn't know what it was. "And so?"

He took a deep breath. "You and I must go to Scotland and find him. Explain. Tell him what's happening." He added, his voice raised as though she were slightly deaf, "Tell him that I don't want to go to Canada with Diana and Shaun."

"You know what he'll say to that, don't you? He'll say what the hell's it got to do with him."

"I don't think he'll say that . . ."

She felt ashamed. "All right. So we go to Scotland and we find Angus. And what do we tell him?"

"That he's got to come back to London and look after me. He can't run away from responsibilities for the rest of his life—that's what Diana's always saying. And I'm a responsibility. That's what I am, a responsibility."

"How could he look after you?"

"We could have a little flat, and he could get a job . . ."

"*Angus?*"

"Why not? Other people do. The only reason he's stuck out against it all this time is because he doesn't want to do anything that Diana wants."

Despite herself Caroline had to smile. "I must say, that fits."

"But for *us* he would come. He says he misses us. He'd like to be with us."

"And how would we get to Scotland? How could we get out of the house without Diana missing us? You know she'd be on the telephone to every airport and railway station. And we can't borrow her car, we'd be flagged down by the first policeman we came to."

"I know," said Jody. "But I've thought it all out." He finished his milk and moved in closer. "I've got a plan."

* * *

27

Although, in a day or so it would be April, the bitter black afternoon was already sinking into darkness. Indeed it had scarcely been light all day. Since morning, the sky had been filled with low and leaden clouds which spilled, every now and then, into thin freezing showers of rain. The countryside was equally bleak. What could be seen of the hills were dark with the last brown grass of the winter. Snow, left over from the last fall, covered most of the high ground and lay deep in haphazard corries and sunless crannies, looking like ineptly applied icing sugar.

Between the hills, the glen took its shape from the twists and turns of the river and down this the wind blew, straight from the north —from the Arctic, possibly—hard and cold and without mercy. It dragged at the bare branches of the trees; tore old dried leaves out of ditches, to fly about, demented, in the bitter air; made a sound in the tall pines that was like the distant thundering of sea.

In the churchyard, it was exposed and without shelter, and the black-clad groups of people stood, hunched against the blast. The starched surplice of the rector flapped and bellied like an ill-set sail, and Oliver Cairney, bare-headed, felt that his cheeks and ears no longer belonged to him and wished that he had thought to wear a second layer of overcoat.

He found that his mind was in a curious state, partly blurred and partly clear as crystal. The words of the service, which should have been meaningful, he scarcely heard, and yet his attention was caught and held by the bright yellow petals of a great bunch of daffodils, flaming on that sombre day like a candle in a dark room. And although most of the mourners who stood about him, just beyond the perimeter of his vision, were as anonymous as shadows, one or two of them had caught his notice, like figures in the foreground of a painting. Cooper, for one, the old keeper, in his best tweed suit and a black knitted tie. And the comforting bulk of Duncan Fraser, neighbour to Cairney. And the girl, the strange girl, incongruous in this homely gathering. A dark girl, very slender and tanned, a black fur hat deep over her ears and her face almost obliterated behind a huge pair of dark glasses. Quite glamorous. Disturbing. Who was she? A friend of Charles? It seemed unlikely . . .

He found himself lost in unworthy speculations, jerked his mind free of them and tried once more to concentrate on what was happening. But the malicious wind, as though taking sides with Oliver's own personal Satan, rose, howling, in a sudden gust, tore a flurry of dead leaves from the ground at his feet and sent them flying. Disturbed, he turned his head, and found himself looking straight at the unknown girl. She had taken off the glasses, and he saw with astonishment that it was Liz Fraser. Liz, unbelievably elegant, standing beside her father. For an instant, his eyes met hers, and then he turned away, his thoughts in a turmoil. Liz, whom he had not seen for two years or more. Liz, grown up now and for some reason, at Rossie Hill. Liz, whom his brother had so adored. He found time to feel grateful to her for coming today. It would have meant everything to Charles.

And then, at last, it was over. People began to move, thankfully, away from the cold, turning their backs on the new grave and the piles of shivering spring flowers. They walked in twos and threes out of the churchyard, blown by the gale, swept through the gate like dust before a broom.

Oliver found himself out on the pavement, shaking hands and making appropriate noises.

"So good of you to come. Yes . . . a tragedy . . ."

Old friends, village people, farmers from the other side of Relkirk, many of whom Oliver had never seen before. Charles's friends. They introduced themselves.

"So good of you to come so far. If you have time on your way home, drop in at Cairney. Mrs Cooper's got a big tea ready . . ."

Now, only Duncan Fraser waited. Duncan, large and solid, buttoned into his black overcoat and mufflered in cashmere, his grey hair blown into a coxcomb. Oliver looked for Liz.

"She's gone," said Duncan. "Went home by herself. Not much good at this sort of thing."

"I'm sorry. But you'll come back to Cairney, Duncan. Have a dram to warm you up."

"Of course I'll come."

The rector materialized at his side. "I won't come to Cairney, Oliver, thank you all the same. My wife's in bed. 'Flu, I think." They shook hands, a silent acknowledgement of thanks on one hand and sympathy on the other. "Let me know what you eventually plan to do."

"I could tell you now only it would take too long."

"Later then, there's plenty of time."

The wind filled his cassock. His hands, holding the prayer book, were swollen and red with cold. Like beef sausages, thought Oliver. He turned and went away from Oliver, up the church path between the leaning gravestones, his white surplice bobbing away through the gloom. Oliver watched until he had gone back into the church and closed the great door behind him, and then he went down the pavement to where his car waited, solitary. He got in and closed the door and sat, glad to be private and alone. Now that the ordeal of the funeral was over, it was possible to accept the idea that Charles was dead. Having accepted this, it seemed likely that things, now, would get easier. Already Oliver felt—not happier, exactly—but calm and able to feel pleased that so many people had come today, and pleased, especially, that Liz had been there.

After a little, he reached awkwardly into his coat pocket, found a packet of cigarettes, took one and lit it. He looked at the empty street and told himself that it was time to go home, there were still the last small social obligations to be met. People would be waiting. He turned on the ignition, put the car into gear and moved out into the street, the frozen gutters crunching beneath the heavy treads of the snow tyres.

By five o'clock the last visitor had gone. Or, at least, the second last visitor. Duncan Fraser's old Bentley still stood by the front door, but then Duncan scarcely qualified as a visitor.

Oliver, having seen the final car away, came back indoors, shut the front door with a slam and returned to the library and the comfort of a roaring fire. As he did this, Lisa, the old Labrador, roused herself and came across the room to his side, and then, realizing that the one for whom she waited had still not come, returned slowly to the hearth-rug and settled down once more. She was—had been—Charles's dog, and somehow her air of being lost and abandoned was the most unbearable thing of all.

He saw that Duncan, left alone, had drawn up a chair to the blaze and made himself comfortable. His face was ruddy, perhaps from the heat of the fire, but more likely from the central heating of the two large whiskies which he had already drunk.

The room, always shabby, bore witness to the remains of Mrs Cooper's excellent tea. Crumbs of fruit-cake littered the white damask cloth spread over the table which had been pushed to the far side of the room. Empty teacups stood about, interspersed with tumblers which had contained something a little stronger than tea.

As he appeared, Duncan looked up and smiled and stretched his legs and said, in a voice still rich with the accents of his native Glasgow, "I should be on my way." He made, however, no move to go, and Oliver, stopping at the table to cut himself a slice of cake, said, "Stay for a bit." He did not want to be left alone. "I want to hear about Liz. Have another drink."

Duncan Fraser eyed his empty glass as though debating the proposition. "Well," he said at last, as Oliver had known that he would; he let Oliver relieve him of the glass. ". . . Maybe a very small one. But you've not had a drink yourself. It would be companionable if you'd join me."

"Yes, I will now."

He took the glass over to the table, found a second, clean one, poured the whisky and added, not too generously, water from a jug. "I didn't recognize her, do you know that? I couldn't think who she was." He carried the glasses back to the fire.

"Yes, she's changed."

"Has she been with you long?"

"A couple of days. Staying in the West Indies with some girlfriend or other. I went over to meet the plane at Prestwick. I hadn't intended going over, but, well . . . I thought it would be better to tell her myself about Charles." He gave the ghost a grin. "You know, women are a funny lot, Oliver. Hard to know what they're thinking. They bottle things up, seem to be afraid to let go."

"But she came today."

"Oh yes, she was there. But this is the first time Liz has ever had to face up to the fact that dying is a thing that happens to people you know, not just names in newspapers and obituary columns. Friends die. Lovers. She'll maybe be down to see you tomorrow or the next day . . . I couldn't say for sure . . ."

"She was the only girl Charles ever looked at. You know that, don't you?"

"Yes. I knew. Even when she was a little girl . . ."

"He was only waiting for her to grow up." Duncan made no reply to this. Oliver found himself a cigarette and lit it, and then let himself down on to the edge of the chair that stood on the other side of the hearth. Duncan eyed him.

"And what are you going to do now? With Cairney I mean?"

"Sell it," said Oliver.

"Just like that."

"Just like that. I have no alternative."

"It's a shame to let a place like this go."

"Yes, but I don't live here. My job and roots are in London. And I was never cut out to be a Scottish laird. That was Charles's job."

"Doesn't Cairney mean anything to you?"

"Of course. The house where I grew up."

"You were always a cool-headed fellow. What do you do with yourself in London? I could never stand the place."

"I love it."

"Are you making money?"

"Enough. For a decent flat, and a car."

Duncan's eyes narrowed. "What about your love life?"

If anyone else had asked Oliver that question he would have thrown something at them for sheer bloody interference. But this was different. *You wily old coot,* thought Oliver, and told him, "Satisfactory."

"I can imagine you, running around with a lot of glamorous women . . ."

"From your tone I can't tell whether you are disapproving or merely envious . . ."

"I never worked it out," Duncan said drily, "how Charles ever got himself a young brother like you. Have you never thought of getting married?"

"I'm not getting married until I'm too old to do anything else."

Duncan gave a wheeze of a laugh. "That puts me in my place. But let's get back to Cairney. If you mean to sell it, will you sell to me?"

"I'd rather sell to you than anyone else. You know that."

"I'll take the farm in with mine, and the moor and the loch. But there'd still be the house. You could maybe sell that separately. After all, it's not too large, nor too far from the road, and the garden is perfectly manageable."

It was comforting to hear him speak this way, putting emotional decisions into practical language, cutting Oliver's problems down to size. But this was the way that Duncan Fraser worked. This was how he had made his money at a comparatively early age, been able to sell up his London business for an astronomical figure and done what he had always wanted to do, which was to return to Scotland, buy some land and settle down to the pleasant life of a country gentleman.

However, this fulfilment of his ambition had its ironic aspect, for Duncan's wife, Elaine, never particularly anxious to leave her native South and put down roots in the wilds of Perthshire, soon became bored with the slow pace of life at Rossie Hill. She missed her friends and the weather got her down. The winters, she complained, were long, cold and dry. The summers, short, cold and wet. Accordingly her flying visits to London became more frequent and of longer duration until the inevitable day came when she announced that she was never going to return, and the marriage broke up.

If Duncan was distressed by this, he managed to hide it very well. He enjoyed having Liz to himself and when she went off to visit her mother, he was never lonely, for his interests were legion. When he had first come to Rossie Hill, local people had been sceptical of his capabilities as a farmer, but he had proved himself—now he was accepted, a member of the club in Relkirk and a J.P. Oliver was very fond of him.

He said, "You make it all sound so reasonable and easy, not like selling one's home at all."

"Well, that's the way things are." The older man finished his drink in a single enormous gulp, laid the glass on the table by his chair and abruptly stood up. "Think about it, anyway. How long are you up for?"

"I've two weeks' leave of absence."

"Suppose we meet on Wednesday in Relkirk? I'll give you lunch and we'll have a chat with the lawyers. Or is that pushing things too fast?"

"Not at all. The sooner it's buttoned up, the better."

"In that case, I'll be taking myself home."

He started for the door and at once Lisa got up and, at a distance, followed them out into the chilly hall, her claws scratching on the polished parquet floor.

Duncan glanced back at her over his shoulder. "It's a sad thing, a dog without a master."

"The worst thing of all."

Lisa watched while Oliver helped Duncan on with his coat and then accompanied them both out to where the old black Bentley waited. The evening was, if possible, colder than ever, black dark and torn with wind. The puddled driveway, beneath their shoes, rang hard with ice.

"We'll have more snow yet," said Duncan.

"Looks like it."

"Any message for Liz?"

"Tell her to come and see me."

"I'll do that. See you Wednesday, then, at the club. Twelve-thirty."

"I'll be there." Oliver shut the car door. "Drive carefully."

When the car had gone he went back indoors with Lisa at his heels and shut the door and stood for a moment, his attention caught by the extraordinary emptiness of the house. This had struck him before—had been striking him at intervals ever since he arrived from London two days before. He wondered if he would ever get used to it.

The hall was cold and quiet. Lisa, worried by Oliver's stillness, pushed her nose into his hand, and he stooped to fondle her head, winding her silky ears over his fingers. The wind buffeted, a draught caught the curtain which hung across the front door, and sent it billowing, a swirling skirt of velvet. Oliver shivered and went back to the library, putting his head around the kitchen door on the way. Presently he was joined by Mrs Cooper with her tray. Together they piled cups and saucers, stacked glasses, cleared the table. Mrs Cooper folded the starched damask cloth and Oliver helped her pull the table back into the middle of the room. Then he followed her back into the kitchen, held the door open so that she could carry through the laden tray, and followed her, with the empty teapot in one hand and the nearly empty whisky bottle in the other.

She began to wash the dishes. He said, "You're tired. Leave them."

She kept her back turned towards him. "Oh, no, I canna leave them. I've never left a single dirty cup for the morning."

"Then go home when you've finished that lot."

"What about your supper?"

"I'm full of fruit cake. I don't want any supper." Her back remained stiff and unrelenting, as though she found it impossible to show any grief. She had adored Charles. Oliver said, "It was good cake." And then he said, "Thank you."

Mrs Cooper did not turn around. Presently, when it became obvious that she was not going to, Oliver went out of the kitchen and back to the library fire, and left her on her own.

3

Behind Diana Carpenter's house in Milton Gardens was a long narrow garden which backed on to a cobbled mews. Between the garden and the mews was a high wall with a gate in it and what had once been a large double garage, but when Diana returned to London from Aphros, she decided that it would be a sound investment to turn the garage into a paying property, and accordingly built over it a small flat for letting. This diversion had kept her busy and happy for a year or more and when it was finished and furnished and totally decorated, she let it at a thumping rent to an American diplomat, posted to London for two years. He was the perfect tenant, but when he was returned to Washington and she started casting about for someone to take his place, she was not so fortunate.

For, out of the past, Caleb Ash turned up with his girlfriend Iris, two guitars, a Siamese cat and nowhere to live.

"And who," asked Shaun, "is Caleb Ash?"

"Oh, he was a friend of Gerald Cliburn's in Aphros. One of those people who are always just on the verge of doing something, like writing a novel or painting a mural, or starting in business or building a hotel. But they never do. Anyway, Caleb's the laziest man in the world."

"And Mrs Ash?"

"Iris. And they're not married."

36

"Don't you want to have them in the flat?"

"No."

"Why not?"

"Because I think they'll be an unsettling influence on Jody."

"Will he remember them?"

"Of course. They were always in and out of our house."

"And you didn't like him?"

"I didn't say that, Shaun. You can't help liking Caleb Ash, he has all the charm in the world. But I don't know, living at the bottom of the garden like that . . ."

"Can they pay the rent?"

"He says so."

"Will they turn the place into a pigsty?"

"Not at all. Iris is very house-proud. Always polishing floors and stirring stews in great copper pots."

"You make my mouth water. Let them have the place. They're friends from the old days, you shouldn't lose all your links, and I don't see how his being there can do Jody any harm at all . . ."

And so Caleb and Iris and the cat and the guitars and the cooking-pots moved into the Stable Cottage, and Diana gave them a little bit of ground to make a garden, and Caleb paved it and grew a camellia in a pot and thus managed, out of nothing, to create a nostalgic Mediterranean ambience.

Jody, naturally enough, adored him, but from the start he was warned by Diana that he must visit Caleb and Iris only when he was invited, otherwise there was the danger that he would make a nuisance of himself. And Katy came out strongly anti-Caleb, especially when, by means of the local grapevine, she latched on to the fact that Caleb and Iris were not married and never likely to be.

"You're not going down the garden to see that Mr Ash again, are you?"

"He asked me, Katy. Sukey the cat's had kittens."

"More of them Siamese things?"

"Well, they aren't, actually. She had an affair with the tabby who lives at number eight in the mews, and they're a sort of mixture. Caleb says they'll stay that way."

Katy busied herself with a kettle. She was put out. "Well, I don't know, I'm sure."

"I thought we might have had one."

"Not one of them nasty yawling things. Anyway, Mrs Carpenter doesn't want no animals around this house. You've heard her often enough. No animals. And a cat is animals so that's that."

The morning after the dinner-party, Caroline and Jody Cliburn emerged from the garden door at the back of the house, and walked down the flagged path towards the Stable Cottage. They made no pretence of concealing themselves. Diana was out and Katy in the kitchen . . . which faced out over the street . . . preparing lunch. They knew, moreover, that Caleb was in, for they had telephoned to ask if they could come over and he had said that he would be waiting for them.

The morning was cold, windy, very bright. The blue sky was reflected in puddles which had collected on the damp paving stones, and the sun was dazzling. It had been a long winter. Now, only the first green stumps of bulbs protruded from the black flowerbeds. All else was brown and withered and seemingly dead.

"Last year," said Caroline, "at this time, there were crocuses. All over the place."

But Caleb's little patch of garden was more sheltered and sunny and there were already daffodils bobbing in his green-painted troughs, and some snowdrops clustered around the base of the sooty-barked almond tree in the middle of the patio.

Access to the flat was by an outside staircase which rose to a wide, decked terrace, rather like the balcony of a Swiss chalet. Caleb had heard their approaching voices, and when they ran up the steps was already out on the balcony to greet them, his hands on the wooden rail, looking like the skipper of some island caique, welcoming guests aboard.

And indeed, he had lived for so many years on Aphros that his features had taken on a strongly Greek cast, much as the faces of people who have been married for many years will grow alike. His eyes were so deep set that it was almost impossible to guess their colour, his face was brown, much lined, his nose a jutting prow, his hair thick and grey and curly. His voice was deep and rich. It always made Caroline think of rough wine and fresh new bread and the smell of garlic in a salad.

"Jody. Caroline." He embraced them, one in each arm, and

38

kissed them both with a wonderfully Greek lack of restraint. No one ever kissed Jody except, sometimes, Caroline. Diana, with her usual perception, guessed how much he hated it. But with Caleb it was different, a respectful salute of affection, man to man.

"What a pleasant surprise! Come along in. I've put the coffee-pot on."

In the days of the American diplomat the little flat had had an air of New England neatness, cool and polished. Now, under Iris's unmistakable influence, it was uncontrived, and colourful; unframed canvases lined the walls, a mobile of coloured glass hung from the ceiling, a Greek shawl had been flung over Diana's carefully chosen chintzes. The room was very warm and smelled of coffee.

"Where's Iris?"

"Out shopping." He pushed up a chair. "Sit down. I'll get the coffee."

Caroline sat down. Jody followed Caleb and presently they returned, Jody carrying a tray with three mugs and the sugar bowl, and Caleb with his coffee-pot. Room was found for all this on a low table in front of the fire, and they settled themselves around it.

"You're not in trouble?" Caleb asked cautiously. He was always wary of getting on the wrong side of Diana.

"Oh no," said Caroline automatically. But, on thought, she amended this. "At least not really."

"Tell me," said Caleb. So Caroline told him. About the letter from Angus and Jody not wanting to go to Canada, and the ideas he had for finding his brother again.

"So we've decided to go to Scotland. Tomorrow. That's Tuesday."

Caleb said. "Are you going to tell Diana?"

"She'd talk us out of it. You know she would. But we'll leave her a letter."

"And Hugh?"

"Hugh would talk me out of it as well."

Caleb frowned. "Caroline, you're meant to be marrying the man in a week."

"I am marrying him."

Caleb said "Hmm" as though he scarcely believed her. He looked down at Jody, sitting beside him. "And you. What about you? What about school?"

"School finished on Friday. This is holidays."

Caleb said "Hmm" again. Caroline became apprehensive. "Caleb, don't you dare to say you don't approve."

"Of course I don't approve. It's an insane idea. If you want to talk to Angus, why don't you telephone?"

"Jody doesn't want to. It's too complicated trying to explain something like this over the telephone."

"And anyway," said Jody, "you can't *persuade* people on the telephone."

Caleb grinned wryly. "You mean you think Angus will take some persuading? I agree with you. You're going to ask him to come to London, set up house, change his entire life style."

Jody ignored this. "So we can't telephone," he said stubbornly.

"And I suppose writing a letter would take too long?"

Jody nodded.

"Telegram?"

Jody shook his head.

"Well, that seems to have taken care of the alternatives. Which brings us to the next point. How are you going to get to Scotland?"

Caroline said, in what she hoped was a winning fashion, "That's one of the reasons, Caleb, we wanted to talk it over with you. You see, we have to have a car, and we can't take Diana's. But if we had your little car, the Mini van, if you could spare it . . . You and Iris? I mean, you don't use it that much and we'll take the most tremendous care of it."

"*My* car? And what am I meant to say when Diana comes storming down the garden with a long string of uncomfortable questions?"

"You could say it had gone to be serviced. It's only a tiny white lie."

"It's more than a white lie, it's tempting Providence. That car's not been serviced since I bought it seven years ago. Suppose it breaks down?"

"We'll risk it."

"And money?"

"I've got enough."

"And when do you reckon on getting back?"

"Thursday, or Friday. With Angus."

"You're hopeful. What if he won't come?"

"We'll cross that bridge when we get to it."

Caleb stood up, restless and undecided. He went to the window to see if Iris was coming, to help him extricate himself from this hideous dilemma. But there was no sign of her. He told himself that these were the children of his best friend. He sighed. "If I agree to help you and if I do lend you my car, it's only because I think it's time for Angus to shoulder a few responsibilities. I think he should come back." He turned to face them. "But I have to know where you're going. The address. How long you'll be . . ."

"The Strathcorrie Arms, Strathcorrie. And if we aren't back by Friday, you can tell Diana where we've gone. But not before."

"All right." Caleb nodded his great head and looked as though he were about to put it into a noose. "It's a deal."

They composed a telegram to Angus.

WE WILL BE AT STRATHCORRIE ON TUESDAY EVENING TO DISCUSS IMPORTANT PLAN WITH YOU LOVE JODY AND CAROLINE.

This done, Jody wrote a letter which would be left behind for Diana.

Dear Diana.

I had a letter from Angus and he is in Scotland so Caroline and I have gone to look for him. We will try to be home by Friday. Please don't worry.

But the letter for Hugh was not so easy and Caroline struggled over its composition for an hour or more.

Dearest Hugh.

As Diana will have told you, Jody had a letter from Angus. He came home from India by sea, and is now working in Scotland. We both feel it is important that we should see him before Jody goes to Canada and so by the time you get this we will be on our way to Scotland. We hope to be back in London on Friday.

I would have discussed it with you but you would have been duty bound to tell Diana and then we should have been talked out of going and would never have seen him. And it is important to us that he knows what is going to happen.

I know it is a terrible thing to do, going off like this the week of our

41

wedding without telling you. But all being well, we'll be home on Friday.

My love,
Caroline.

By the Tuesday morning, the first fine flurry of snow had fallen and then stopped, leaving the ground speckled like the feathers of a hen. The wind, however, had not let up at all, the cold was still extreme and from the look of the lowering, khaki-coloured sky, there was worse weather to come.

Oliver Cairney took one look at it, and decided that it was a good day to stay indoors and try and sort out some of Charles's affairs. It proved a poignant business. Charles, efficient and painstaking, had neatly filed every letter and document relevant to the working of the farm. Tying up the estate was going to be simpler than he had feared.

But there were other things as well. Personal things. Letters and invitations, an out-of-date passport, hotel bills and photographs, Charles's address book, his diary, the silver fountain pen he had been given for his twenty-first, a bill from his tailor.

Oliver remembered his mother's voice, reading aloud a poem to them; Alice Duer Miller.

What do you do with a woman's shoes.
After a woman is dead?

Steeling himself, he tore up the letters, sorted the photographs, threw away stubs of sealing wax, ends of string, a broken lock without a key, a dried-up bottle of India ink. By the time the clock struck eleven, the wastepaper basket was overflowing and he had just got up to collect the rubbish and cart it out into the kitchen when he heard the slam of the front door. It was half-glassed and made a cavernous sound which echoed around the panelled hall. Carrying the wastepaper basket, he went out to see who it was, and came face to face with Liz Fraser walking down the passage towards him.

"Liz."

She wore trousers and a short fur coat; the same black hat that she had worn yesterday, pulled deep over her ears. As he watched, she took it off and with the other hand ruffled up her short dark hair. It was an oddly nervous, uncertain gesture, entirely at odds with her sleek appearance. Her face was rosy from the cold and she was smiling. She looked marvellous.

"Hallo, Oliver."

She reached his side, leaned over the mound of crumpled paper to kiss his cheek. She said, "If you don't want to see me, say so, and I'll go away again."

"Who said I didn't want to see you?"

"I thought maybe—"

"Well, don't think maybe. Come and I'll make you a cup of coffee. I need one myself and I'm tired of being on my own."

He led the way towards the kitchen, pushing the swing-door open with the seat of his pants, letting her go ahead of him, with her long legs and her fresh, open-air smell all mingled up with Chanel No. 5. "Put the kettle on," he told her. "I'll go and get rid of this lot."

He went through the kitchen, out of the back door and into the bitter cold, managed to get his load out of the wastepaper basket and into the dustbin without too much of it blowing away, crammed the lid back on the dustbin and returned thankfully to the warmth of the kitchen. Liz, looking incongruous, was at the sink, filling the kettle from the tap.

Oliver said, "My God, it's cold!"

"I know and this is meant to be spring. I walked over from Rossie Hill and I thought I would die." She carried the kettle over to the Aga, lifted the heavy lid, and placed the kettle on the hob. She stayed by the stove, turning to lean against its warmth. Across the room they faced each other. Then they spoke at the same time.

"You've had your hair cut," said Oliver.

"I'm sorry about Charles," said Liz.

They both stopped, waiting for the other to go on. Then Liz said, looking confused, "I had it done for swimming. I've been staying with this friend in Antigua."

"I wanted to thank you for coming yesterday."

"I . . . I've never been to a funeral before."

Her eyes, ringed with eye-liner and black mascara, were suddenly bright with unshed tears. The short, elegant haircut exposed the length of her neck and the clear line of the determined chin that she had inherited from her father. As he watched, she began to undo the buttons of her fur coat, and her hands were brown too, the almond-shaped nails painted a very pale pink, and she wore a thick gold signet ring and a cluster of fine gold bracelets on one slender wrist.

He said, inadequately, "Liz, you've grown up."

"Of course. I'm twenty-two now. Had you forgotten?"

"How long is it since I've seen you?"

"Five years? It's five years at least."

"What's happened to the time?"

"You were in London. I went to Paris, and every time I came back to Rossie Hill, you were always away."

"But Charles was here."

"Yes. Charles was here." She fiddled with the lid of the kettle. "But if Charles ever noticed my appearance, he certainly never remarked on it."

"He noticed all right. He was just never very good at saying what he felt. Anyway, to Charles you were always perfect. Even when you were fifteen with pigtails and bulging jeans. He was only waiting for you to grow up."

She said, "I can't believe he's dead."

"I couldn't either, until yesterday. But I think I've accepted it now." The kettle began to sing. He left the side of the stove and went to find mugs and a jar of instant coffee and a bottle of milk from the fridge. Liz said, "Father told me about Cairney."

"You mean about selling up?"

"How can you bear to, Oliver?"

"Because there's no other choice."

"Even the house? Does the house have to go?"

"What would I do with the house?"

"You could keep it. Use it for week-ends and holidays, just to keep a root in Cairney."

"That sounds like an extravagance to me."

"Not really." She hesitated slightly and then went on in a rush. "When you're married and have children, you can bring them here, and they can do all the lovely things you used to do. Run wild, and build houses in the beech tree, and have ponies . . ."

"Who said I was thinking of getting married?"

"Father said that you said that you weren't going to get married until you were too old to do anything else."

"Your father tells you a lot too much."

"And what's that supposed to mean?"

"He always did. He indulged you and let you in on all his secrets. You were a spoiled little brat, did you know that?"

She was amused. "Them's fighting words, Oliver."

"I don't know how you've survived. An only child with two doting parents who didn't even live together. And if that wasn't enough, you always had Charles, spoiling you rotten."

The kettle boiled, and he went over to pick it up. Liz lowered the lid back on to the hotplate. She said, "But you never spoiled me, Oliver."

"I had more sense." He poured the water into the mugs.

"You never took any notice of me at all. You were always telling me to get out from under your feet."

"Ah, but that was when you were a little girl, before you became so glamorous. Incidentally, you know, I didn't recognize you yesterday. It was only when you took off your dark glasses that I realized who it was. Gave me quite a turn."

"Is that coffee ready?"

"Yes, it is. Come and drink it up before it gets cold."

They sat, facing each other across the scrubbed kitchen table. Liz held the mug in her hands as though her fingers were still cold. Her expression was provocative.

"We were talking about you getting married."

"I wasn't."

"How long are you staying at Cairney?"

"Until everything's been tied up. And you?"

Liz shrugged. "I'm meant to be south now. My mother and Parker are in London for a few days on business. I called her when I got back from Prestwick—to tell her about Charles. She tried to make me say I'd go back to them, but I explained that I wanted to be at the funeral."

"You still haven't told me how long you're staying at Rossie Hill."

"I haven't any plans, Oliver."

"Then stay for a little."

"Do you want me to?"

"Yes."

To have this settled and said somehow broke down the last of the tension between them. They sat on, talking, time forgotten. It wasn't until the clock in the hall struck twelve that Liz's attention was distracted. She looked at her watch. "Heavens, is that really the time? I must go."

"What for?"

"Lunch. Remember that quaint old-fashioned meal or have you stopped eating it?"

"Not at all."

"Come back with me now and you can eat it with my father and I."

"I'll drive you home but I won't stay for lunch."

"Why not?"

"I've wasted half the morning already, gossiping with you, and there's the hell of a lot to be done."

"Dinner, then. Tonight?"

He considered this and then, for various reasons, rejected the invitation. "But would tomorrow do?"

She shrugged, easy, the epitome of feminine pliancy. "Whenever."

"Tomorrow would be great. About eight o'clock?"

"A little earlier if you want a drink."

"OK. A little earlier. Now, put your hat and coat on and I'll drive you home."

His car was dark green, small, and low and very fast. She sat beside him with her hands deep in the pockets of her coat, staring ahead at the bleak Scottish countryside and so physically aware of the man beside her that it almost hurt.

He had changed, and yet he had not changed. He was older. There were lines on his face that had not been there before, and an expression in the back of his eyes that made her feel as though she was embarking on an affair with a total stranger. But it was still Oliver; offhand, refusing to commit himself, invulnerable.

For Liz, it had always been Oliver. Charles had merely been the excuse to haunt Cairney, and Liz had shamelessly used him as such, because he had encouraged her constant visits, had always been glad to see her. But it was because of Oliver that she had gone.

Charles was the homely one, stringy and sandy and freckled. But Oliver was glamour. Charles had time and patience for a gawky teenager; time to teach her how to cast a line, serve at tennis; time to nurse her through the agonies of her first grown-up dance, show her how to dance the reels. And all the time she had eyes for no one but Oliver, and had prayed that he would dance with her.

But of course he hadn't. There was always someone else, some strange girl or other invited up from the south. *I met her at University, at a party, staying with old so-and-so.* Over the years there were a great many of them. Oliver's girls were a local joke, but Liz did not think it was funny. Liz had watched from the side-lines and hated them all, mentally making wax images of them and spearing them with pins, wracked as she was with the miseries of teenage jealousy.

And after her parents' separation, it was Charles who wrote to Liz, giving her all the news of Cairney and keeping her in touch. But it was Oliver's photograph, a tiny crooked snapshot she had taken herself, which lived in the secret pocket of her wallet and went everywhere with her.

Now, sitting beside him, she allowed her gaze to move fractionally sideways. Oliver's hands on the leather-bound driving-wheel were long-fingered, square-nailed. There was a scar near his thumb, and she remembered how he had torn his hand open on a new barbed-wire fence. Her eyes moved casually up the length of his arm. His sheepskin collar was turned up and around his neck, touching the dark, thick hair. And then he felt her gaze and turned his head to smile at her, and his eyes, beneath the dark brows, were as blue as speedwells.

He said, "You'll know me next time," but Liz did not reply. She remembered flying in to Prestwick, her father waiting to meet her. *Charles has been killed.* There had been a terrible moment of disbelief, as though firm ground had fallen away, and she was left staring down into a huge, gaping hole. And then, "Oliver?" she had asked faintly.

"Oliver's at Cairney. Or should be by now. Driving up from London today. The funeral's on Monday . . ."

Oliver's at Cairney. Charles, dear, kind, patient Charles, was dead, but Oliver was alive and Oliver was at Cairney. After all these years she would see him again . . . Driving back to Rossie Hill, this thought was never out of her mind. *I'll see him. Tomorrow I'll see him and the next day and the day after that.* And she had called her mother in London and told her about Charles, but when Elaine had tried to persuade her to leave all the sadness behind and come south, to be with her, Liz had refused. The excuse came pat.

"I must stay. Father . . . and the funeral . . ." But all the time she knew, and revelled in the fact, that she was only staying for Oliver.

* * *

And, miraculously, it had worked out. She had known that it would from the moment that Oliver, for no apparent reason, had suddenly turned in the churchyard and looked straight into her face. She had seen it then, first surprise, and then admiration. Oliver was no longer in a position of superiority. Now they were equals. And . . . which was sad, but made everything a great deal simpler . . . there was no longer Charles to be considered. Kind Charles, maddening Charles, always there, like a rusty old dog, waiting to be taken for a walk.

She let her busy, practical mind speed ahead, allowed herself the luxury of indulging in one or two pretty images of the future. It all worked out so neatly that it might have been pre-contrived. A wedding at Cairney, perhaps, a little country wedding in the local church, with just a few friends. Then a honeymoon in . . . ? Antigua would be perfect. Then back to London—he already had a flat in London so they could use that as a base for further house-hunting. And, brilliant idea, she would get her father to give her Cairney house as a wedding present, and the casual suggestions she had put in Oliver's way this morning would, after all, come true. She saw them driving up for long week-ends, spending summer holidays here, bringing children, having house-parties . . .

Oliver said, "You're very quiet all of a sudden."

Liz came back to reality with a bang, saw that they were already nearly home. The car swept up the drive beneath the beeches. Above, bare branches creaked in the cruel wind. They swung around the curve of the gravel to come to a halt in front of the big door.

"I was thinking," said Liz. "Just thinking. Thank you for bringing me home."

"Thank you for coming over to cheer me up."

"And you're coming for dinner tomorrow? Wednesday."

"I shall look forward to it."

"A quarter to eight?"

"A quarter to eight."

They smiled, conveying their mutual pleasure with the arrangement. Then he leaned across to open her door, and Liz got out of the car, and ran up the icy steps and into the shelter of the porch. Here, she turned to wave him away, but Oliver had already departed, and only the back end of his car could be seen, disappearing down the drive, on its way back to Cairney.

* * *

That evening, when Liz was in her bath, she was interrupted by a telephone call from London. Wrapped in a bath-towel she went to take it, and heard her mother's voice on the other end of the line.

"Elizabeth?"

"Hallo, Mummy."

"Darling, how are you? How is everything?"

"It's fine. Perfect. Wonderful."

This lilting reply was not exactly what Elaine had expected. She sounded puzzled. "But did you go to the funeral?"

"Oh, yes, that was ghastly, I hated every moment of it."

"Then why not come south . . . we're here for a few more days . . ."

"I can't come yet . . ." Liz hesitated. Usually she behaved like a clam over her own affairs. Elaine continually complained that she never knew what was going on in her only daughter's life. But all at once Liz felt expansive. The excitement of what had happened today and what might be going to happen tomorrow was getting the better of her, and she knew that if she did not talk about Oliver to someone, then she was going to burst.

She finished the sentence in a burst of confidence.

". . . the thing is, Oliver's here for a bit. And he's coming over for dinner tomorrow night."

"Oliver? Oliver Cairney?"

"Yes, of course Oliver Cairney. What other Oliver do we know?"

"You mean . . . ? Because of Oliver . . ."

"Yes. Because of *Oliver.*" Liz laughed. "Oh, Mummy, don't be so dense."

"But I always thought it was Ch . . ."

"Well, it wasn't," said Liz quickly.

"And what has Oliver got to say to all this?"

"Well, I don't think he's exactly displeased."

"Well, I don't know . . ." Elaine sounded confused. "It's the last thing I ever expected, but if you're happy . . ."

"Oh, I am. I am happy. Believe me, I've never been so happy."

Her mother said, faintly, "Well, let me know what happens."

"I will."

"And let me know when you come south . . ."

49

"We'll probably come together," said Liz, already imagining it. "Perhaps we'll drive down together."

Her mother rang off at last. Liz laid down the receiver, wrapped the bath-towel more firmly around herself and padded back to the bathroom. Oliver. She said his name, over and over. Oliver Cairney. She got back into the bath and turned on the hot tap with her toe. Oliver.

Driving north was like driving backwards in time. Spring was late everywhere, but in London there had at least been traces of green, an incipient leafiness on the trees in the park, the first stars of yellow crocus in the park. Daffodils and purple iris flowered from pavement stalls, and there were displays of mouth-melting summer clothes in the big shop windows, making one think of holidays and cruises and blue skies and sun.

But the motorway cut north like a ribbon through flat country that grew progressively more grey and cold and apparently unproductive. The roads were wet and dirty. Every passing lorry—and Caleb's old car was passed by practically everything—threw up blinding showers of wet brown mud that smothered the windscreen and forced the wipers to work overtime. To add to their discomfort, none of the windows seemed to fit properly and the heater was either faulty or needed some secret adjustment which neither Jody nor Caroline could master. Whatever the reason, it did not work.

Despite all this, Jody was in the highest of spirits. He read the map, sang, did complicated sums to work out their speed average (sadly low) and their mileage.

We're a third of the way there. We're half-way there. and then, "In another five miles we'll be at Scotch Corner. I wonder why it's called Scotch Corner when it's not even in Scotland?"

"Perhaps people get out there, and buy themselves scotches?"

Jody thought this very funny. "We've never been to Scotland, any of us. I wonder why Angus came to Scotland?"

"When we find him we'll ask him."

"Yes," said Jody cheerfully, thinking about seeing Angus. He leaned back for the rucksack that they had prudently filled with food. He opened it and looked inside. "What would you like now? There's a ham sandwich left and a rather bruised-looking apple and some chocolate biscuits."

"I'm all right. I don't want anything."

"Do you mind if I eat the ham sandwich?"

"Not at all."

After Scotch Corner they took the A68, the small car grinding up over the bleak moors of Northumberland, through Otterburn and so on to Carter Bar. The road wound upwards, looping to and fro against the steep gradient, and then they crested the final hill and passed the border stone, and Scotland lay before them.

"We're there," said Jody in tones of the greatest satisfaction. But Caroline saw only a spread of undulating grey country, and in the distance hills that were white with snow.

She said, in some apprehension, "You don't suppose it's going to snow, do you? It's terribly cold."

"Oh, not at this time of the year."

"What about those hills?"

"That'll be left over from the winter. It's just not melted."

"The sky looks terribly dark."

It did. Jody frowned. "Would it matter if it snowed?"

"I don't know. But we haven't got snow tyres and I've never driven in really bad weather."

After a little, "Oh, it'll be all right," said Jody, and took up his map again. "Now the next place we've got to get to is Edinburgh."

By then it was nearly dark, the windy city spangled with street lights. Inevitably, they got lost, but finally found the correct one-way street and headed out on the motorway towards the bridge. They stopped, for the last time, for petrol and oil. Caroline got out of the car to stretch her legs while the garage attendant checked the water and then attacked the dirty windscreen with a damp sponge. As he did this, he observed the worn, travelled little car with some interest, and then turned his attention to its occupants.

"Have you come far?"

"From London."

"Are you going on?"

"We're going to Strathcorrie. In Perthshire."

"You've a long way to go."

"Yes. We know."

"You'll be driving into some dirty weather." Jody liked the way he said dirty. Durrty. He practised saying it, under his breath.

"Will we?"

51

"Aye. I just heard the weather forecast. More snow. You'll need to watch. Your tyres . . ."—he kicked them with the toe of his boot—"your tyres are no' all that good."

"We'll be all right."

"Well, if you get stuck in the snow, remember the golden rule. Don't get out of the car."

"We'll remember."

They paid him and thanked him and set off once more. And the garage man watched them go, shaking his head at the irresponsibility of all Sassenachs.

The Forth Bridge reared ahead of them, with warning lights flashing. SLOW. STRONG WINDS. They paid their toll and drove out and over it, slammed and battered by the wind. On the far side, the motorway cut north, but it was so dark and stormy that, beyond the headlights' feeble beam, they could see nothing.

"What a shame," said Jody. "Here we are in Scotland and we can't see a thing. Not so much as a haggis."

But Caroline couldn't even rustle up a laugh. She was cold and tired and anxious about the weather and the threatened snow. Suddenly the adventure was an adventure no longer, but simply an act of the greatest possible folly.

The snow began to fall as they left Relkirk behind them. Blown by the wind it came at them out of the darkness in long streaks of blinding white.

"Like flak," said Jody.

"Like what?"

"Flak. Anti-aircraft fire. In war films. That's what it looks like."

At first, it did not lie on the road. But later, climbing up into the hills, it became quite deep, piled in ditches and on dykes, blown by the wind into great pillow-like drifts. It stuck to the windscreen, and piled up beneath the wipers until they stopped working altogether and Caroline had to stop the car, and Jody got out and, with an old glove, wiped the snow from the glass. He got back into the car, wet and shivering.

"It's all in my shoes. It's freezing."

They moved forward again. "How many more miles?" Her mouth was dry with fright, her fingers clamped to the steering-wheel. They appeared to be in a country quite empty of any sort of habitation. Not a light showed, not another car, not even a track on the road.

Jody turned on the torch and studied his map. "About eight, I would say. Strathcorrie's about eight miles."

"And what time is it?"

He looked at his watch. "Half past ten."

Presently they topped a small rise and the road ran downhill, narrow between high dykes. Caroline changed down and as they gathered speed, braked gently, but not gently enough, and the car lurched into a skid. For a terrible instant she knew that she was out of control. A dyke reared up before them, and then the front wheels thumped into a bank of snow and the car came to a dead stop. In trepidation Caroline started up the engine again, managed to turn the wheels out of the drift, and back the car on to the road. They moved on at a snail's pace.

"Is it dangerous?" asked Jody.

"Yes. I think it probably is. If only we had snow tyres."

"Caleb wouldn't have snow tyres, even if he lived in the Arctic."

They were now in a deep glen, tree-lined and running alongside a steep gorge. From this came the sound of a river, purling and splashing above the sound of the wind. They came to a hump-backed bridge, very steep and blind, and, frightened of sticking on its slope, Caroline took it in a small burst of speed, and then saw, too late, that beyond it the road took a sharp turn to the right. Ahead were drifts, and the blank face of a stone wall.

She heard Jody gasp. She spun the wheel, but it was too late. The little car, suddenly with a mind of its own, headed straight for the wall, and then plunged nose-first into a deep ditch full of snow. The engine stalled instantly, and they finished up at an angle of forty-five degrees with the back wheels still on the road, and the headlights and the radiator buried deep in snow.

It was dark without the headlights. Caroline put out a hand to switch them off and then turn off the ignition. She was shaking. She turned to Jody. "Are you all right?"

"I bumped my head a bit, that's all."

"I'm sorry."

"You couldn't help it."

"Perhaps we should have stopped before now. Perhaps we should have stayed in Relkirk."

Jody peered at the swirling darkness. He said, bravely, "You know, I think this is a blizzard. I've never been in a blizzard. The man at the garage said we had to stay in the car."

"We can't. It's much too cold. You wait here, I'm going to look."

"Don't get lost."

"Give me the torch."

She buttoned up her coat, and gingerly got out of the car, falling knee-deep into a snow drift, and then clambering up on to the firm surface of the road. It was wet and bitterly cold and even with the torch to guide her, the snow was blinding, confusing. It would be easy to lose all sense of direction.

She took a few paces down the road, shining the torch along the stone wall which had proved their undoing. It carried on for about ten yards and then curved inwards to form some sort of an entrance. Caroline followed it, and came to a gate post and a wooden gate, open. There was a notice. Screwing her eyes against the snow she turned the beam of the torch upwards and read, with difficulty, CAIRNEY HOUSE. PRIVATE.

She switched off the torch and stared up into the darkness which lay beyond the gate. There seemed to be an avenue of trees, she could hear the thunder of wind in bare branches, high above, and then through the swirl of snowflakes, glimpsed, distantly, a single light.

She turned and went hurrying, floundering back to Jody. She pulled the car door open. "We're in luck."

"How?"

"This wall, it's an estate, or a farm or something. There's a sort of entrance and a gate and a drive. And you can see a light. It can't be more than half a mile."

"But the man at the garage said we had to stay in the car."

"If we stay, we'll die of cold. Come on, the snow's thick, but we can make it. It shouldn't be too long a walk. Leave the rucksack, just get our bags. And button up your jacket. It's cold and we're going to get wet."

He did as she told him, struggling out of the car against its awkward angle. She knew that the important thing was to waste no time. Dressed for London in the spring, they were neither of them prepared for these Arctic conditions. Both were in jeans and thin shoes, Caroline had a suède jacket and a cotton scarf to tie around her head, but Jody's blue anorak was sadly inadequate and his head was bare.

"Do you want the scarf for your head?" The words were torn from her mouth by the wind.

He was furious. "No, of course not."

"Can you carry your bag?"

"Yes, of course I can."

She shut the door. Already the car had collected a considerable coating of snow, its outlines were blurred, soon it would be buried and hidden completely.

"Will anyone drive into it?" Jody asked.

"I don't think so. Anyway, there's nothing we can do. If we left a light on, the snow would simply cover it." She took his hand. "Now come along, we mustn't talk, we've got to hurry."

She led him back to the gate, following the wavering track of her own footprints. Beyond the gate the darkness swept ahead into a black tunnel shimmering with snow. But the light was there still, a pin prick, no more. Far ahead. Hand in hand, heads bent against the wind, they started to walk towards it.

It was a frightening business. All the elements were against them. In moments they were both soaked to the skin and very cold. The overnight bags, which had seemed so light, became heavier with every step. Snow cascaded on to them wet, sodden, clinging like paste. Overhead, high above the snow, the arched branches of leafless trees soughed and creaked ominously, flayed by the wind. Every now and then came the sound of a branch breaking, followed by the crash and splinter of its fall.

Jody was trying to say something. "I hope . . ." His lips were frozen, his teeth chattered, but he struggled to get the words out. "I hope a tree doesn't fall on us."

"So do I."

"And my coat's supposed to be showerproof." His voice was testy. "I'm wet right through."

"This is a blizzard, Jody, not a shower."

The light still shone, perhaps a little brighter, and a little closer to hand, but by now Caroline felt as if they had been walking for ever. It was like an endless journey in a nightmare, with the will-o'-the-wisp light dancing ahead of them, always just out of reach. She had begun to give up hope of ever getting anywhere, when all at once the darkness became a little less dense, the sound of the creaking branches fell behind them, and she realized that they had reached the end of the avenue. At this moment the light disappeared, behind a looming bulk of what was probably a clump of rhododendrons. But as they picked their way around this, the light appeared once more, and now it was quite close. They went forward and stumbled over the edge of a bank. Jody nearly fell and Caroline pulled him to his feet.

"It's all right. We're on a lawn, or grass. Perhaps part of a garden."

"Let's go on," said Jody. It was all he could manage.

Now, the light took shape, shining from an upstairs, uncurtained window. They were walking across an open space towards a house. It reared up ahead of them, made shapeless by the blurring edges of the snow, but they could make out other lights, faintly glowing behind thickly drawn curtains in the downstairs rooms.

"It's a big house," whispered Jody.

It was, too. "All the more room for us," said Caroline, but she did not know if Jody heard. She let go of his hand and fumbled clumsily, frozen fingered, in her pocket for the torch. She turned it on, and the faint beam picked out a flight of stone steps, cushioned in snow, leading to the dark recesses of a square porch. They went up the steps and found themselves in cover, out of the snow. The torch's beam played over the panels of the door, and picked out a long, wrought-iron bell-pull. Caroline put down her bag and reached out to pull it. It was stiff and heavy and apparently produced no result at all. She tried again, lending a little more weight to her efforts, and this time a bell rang, distantly, hollowly, from the back of the house.

"That's working, at any rate." She turned to Jody and inadvertently the torch's beam caught his face and she saw that he was grey with cold, his hair plastered to his skull, his teeth chattering. She switched off her torch and put an arm around him and drew him close. "It'll be all right."

"I hope," said Jody in a distinct voice that shook with nerves. "I hope that a horrible butler doesn't come and say 'You rang, sir?' like they do in horror films."

Caroline hoped so too. She was about to ring the bell again, when she heard the footsteps. A dog barked and a deep voice told it to be quiet. Lights sprang from the narrow windows on either side of the entrance, the footsteps came closer and the next moment the door was flung open and a man stood, just inside, with a yellow labrador, bristling, at his heels.

He said to the dog, "Be quiet, Lisa," and then looked up. "Yes?"

Caroline opened her mouth to speak, but could think of nothing to say. She simply stood there, with one arm around Jody, and perhaps it was the best thing she could have done, for without another word being uttered, her bag had been picked up off the flagged floor, the pair of them had been swept indoors, and then the great door was closed against the stormy night.

The nightmare was over. The house felt warm. They were safe.

4

In his state of astonishment, the thing that struck Oliver more forcibly than anything else was their extreme youth. What were two children doing, at half past eleven, out on a night like this? Where had they come from with their little overnight bags, and where on God's earth were they going? But as the questions crowded into his mind, he realized that they would have to be shelved till later. The only important thing now, was to get them out of their wet clothes and into a hot bath before they both died of exposure.

Without wasting time on explanations he said, "Come along. Quickly." And turned and headed, two at a time, up the stairs. After an instant's hesitation he heard them follow him, hurrying to keep up. His mind raced ahead. There were two bathrooms. He went first to his own, snapped on the light, put the plug in the bath, turned on the hot tap, took time to be thankful that one of the things that really worked in this old house was the hot water system, for almost immediately the steam rolled up in comforting clouds.

"You go in here," he told the girl. "Get in as fast as you can, and stay there till you're warm again. And you—" he took hold of the boy's arm, passive beneath the soggy chill of his clothes—"you come this way." He jostled him back down the long passage to the old nursery bathroom, turning on lights as he went. This bathroom had not been used for some time, but the hot pipes kept it cosy and he drew the old faded curtains, with their pattern of Beatrix Potter characters, and turned on the second set of taps.

The boy was already fumbling with the buttons of his jacket. "Can you manage?"

"Yes, thank you."

"I'll be back."

"All right."

He left the boy to his own devices. Outside the door he stood for a moment, trying to decide what had to be done next. It was obvious that at this time of night they would have to stay until morning, so he went back down the passage to the big old spare bedroom. It was bitterly cold, but he drew the heavy curtains and turned on both bars of the electric fire and then turned down the bedspread and saw with relief that Mrs Cooper had left the double bed made up, with the best linen sheets and hemstitched pillowcases. A door from this room led into a smaller one, once a dressing-room, which contained a single bed, and this too was ready for an occupant, although again the atmosphere was frigid. When he had drawn the curtains and turned on another fire, he returned downstairs, picked up the two small pieces of luggage which had been abandoned in the hall, and carried them along to the library. The fire was dying. He had been on the point of going to bed when the bell disturbed him. But now he built this up, piling on the logs, and then placed a brass-railed fireguard in front of the spitting sparks.

He unzipped the first bag and took out a pair of blue and white striped pyjamas, some slippers, a grey woollen dressing-gown. Everything was slightly damp, so feeling like a conscientious Nanny, he draped them over the fireguard to dry. The other bag produced nothing so practical as blue and white pyjamas. There were bottles and jars, a hairbrush and comb, a pair of little gold slippers, and finally, a nightdress with a matching negligee; pale blue, very lacy, entirely useless. Oliver laid the nightdress alongside the pyjamas. It struck him as looking both suggestive and sexy and he found time to grin at the idea before heading for the kitchen and the business of finding something sustaining for his visitors to eat.

Mrs Cooper had made a pot of scotch broth for Oliver's supper and there was still half of this left. He put it on the Aga to heat, and then remembered that small boys did not always like scotch broth, so he found a tin of tomato soup, and opened that and put it in another saucepan. He took out a tray, cut bread and butter, found some apples, a jug of milk. He considered this homely repast, and then added a whisky bottle (for himself if no one else) and a soda syphon and three tumblers. Finally, he boiled up the big kettle and after a search ran a couple of hot water bottles to earth in an unsuspected drawer. With these, fatly-filled, held under his arm, he went to collect the night-things, which were dry now, and warm, and smelt comforting, like an old-fashioned nursery. He put the bottles in the bed, and then went to his own room and took a shetland sweater from a drawer and a Viyella dressing-gown from the back of the door. Then he found a couple of bath-towels.

He thumped at the bathroom door with his fist. "How are you getting on?"

"I'm warm. It's marvellous," came the girl's voice.

"Well, I'll leave a towel and some things to put on, outside the door. You get dressed when you're good and ready."

"All right."

He did not bother to knock on the door of the other bathroom, but simply opened it and went in. They boy lay in the deep water, slowly moving his legs to and fro. He looked up, unembarrassed by Oliver's abrupt appearance.

"How do you feel now?" asked Oliver.

"Much better, thank you. I'd never been so cold in my life."

Oliver pulled up a chair, and settled himself companionably.

"What happened?" he asked.

The boy sat up in the bath. Oliver saw the freckles, across his back, down his arms, spattered all over his face. His hair was damp and tousled and the colour of copper beech leaves. He said, "The car went into a ditch."

"In the snow?"

"Yes. We came over the little bridge and we didn't know the road turned so quickly. We couldn't see in the snow."

"It's a bad corner at the best of times. What happened to the car?"

"We left it there."

"Where were you going?"

"Strathcorrie."

"And where have you come from?"

"London."

"*London?*" Oliver could not keep the astonishment out of his voice. "From London? Today?"

"Yes. We left early this morning."

"And the girl? Is she your sister?"

"Yes."

"Was she driving?"

"Yes, she drove all the way."

"Just the two of you."

The boy looked dignified. He said, "We were all right."

"Yes, of course," Oliver assured him hastily. "It's just that your sister doesn't look old enough to drive a car."

"She's twenty."

"Well, in that case of course she is old enough."

A small silence followed. Jody took up a sponge, thoughtfully squeezed it and then dabbed at his face, pushing a crest of wet hair off his forehead. He emerged from behind the sponge and said, "I think I'm hot enough now. I think I'll get out."

"Out you come then." Oliver reached for the bath-towel, shook out its folds, and as the boy stepped out on to the bath-mat, wrapped him in it. The boy faced him. Their eyes were level. Oliver gently rubbed at him with the towel.

"What's your name?" he asked.

"Jody."

"Jody what?"

"Jody Cliburn."

"And your sister?"

"She's Caroline."

Oliver took up a handful of towel and rubbed at Jody's hair. "Did you have any particular reason for going to Strathcorrie?"

"My brother's there."

"Is he called Cliburn, too?"

"Yes. Angus Cliburn."

"Ought I to know him?"

"I don't suppose so. He's only been there a little while. He's working in the hotel."

"I see."

"He's going to be rather worried," Jody said.

"Why?" Oliver reached for the pyjamas, held the jacket out for Jody.

"These are all warm," said Jody.

"They've been in front of the fire. Why is your brother going to be worried?"

"We sent him a telegram. He'll be expecting us. And now we aren't there."

"He'll know about the blizzard. He'll guess something like this has happened."

"We never thought it would snow. In London there are crocuses and things and buds on the trees."

"This is the far, frozen North, my boy. You can never depend on the weather."

"I've never been to Scotland before." Jody pulled on his pyjama trousers and tied the cord around his waist. "Neither has Caroline."

"It was bad luck, the weather doing this to you."

"It was rather exciting, really. An adventure."

"Adventures are all very well when they're safely over. But they're not so funny when they're going on. I think you've come out of yours very well."

"We were lucky to find you."

"Yes, I think you were."

"Is this your house?"

"Yes."

"Do you live here all alone?"

"At the moment I do."

"What's it called?"

"Cairney."

"And what's your name."

"The same. Cairney. Oliver Cairney."

"Goodness."

Oliver grinned. "Muddling, isn't it? Now, if you're ready we'll go and find your sister and then get something to eat." He opened the door. "Incidentally, would you rather have scotch broth or tomato soup?"

"Tomato, if you've got it."

"I thought you would."

As they came down the passage, Caroline emerged from the other bathroom. In Oliver's dressing-gown she was submerged. She looked even smaller and thinner than his first impression of her. Her long hair was damp, and the high collar of his sweater appeared to be supporting her fragile head.

"I feel quite different now . . . thank you so much . . ."

"We're going to find something to eat . . ."

"I'm afraid we're being the most terrible nuisance."

"You'll only be a nuisance if you catch colds on me and I'm forced to look after you."

He went on downstairs, and behind him, heard her brother say to Caroline in tones of the greatest satisfaction, "He says it's *tomato* soup."

At the kitchen door he stopped. "That's the library door down there. You go and wait and I'll bring you your supper. And put more logs on the fire, get a good blaze going."

The soup was bubbling gently. He ladled out two bowls, and then carried the laden tray along to the library where he found them by the fire, Jody sitting on a footstool and his sister kneeling on the hearth-rug trying to dry her hair. Lisa, Charles's dog, sat between them, her head resting on Jody's knee. The boy stroked her ears. He looked up as Oliver appeared.

"What's the dog's name?"

"Lisa. Has she made friends with you?"

"I think so."

"She doesn't usually make friends as quickly as that." He put the tray down on a low table, shoving aside some magazines and old newspapers to make room for it.

"Is she your dog?"

"At the moment she is. Have you got a dog?"

"No." His voice was bleak. Oliver decided to change the subject. "Why not have the soup before it gets cold?" And while they started in on their meal, he took away the fireguard, put on another log, poured himself a whisky and soda, and settled in the old sagging arm-chair by the side of the hearth.

They ate in silence. Jody had soon finished his soup, eaten all the bread and butter, drunk a couple of tumblers of milk and then started in on the apples; but his sister only ate a little of her broth and then laid down the spoon as if she were no longer hungry.

"Not nice?" Oliver asked.

"Delicious. But I couldn't eat any more."

63

"Aren't you hungry? You have to be hungry."

Jody chipped in. "She never is."

"A drink, perhaps?"

"No, thank you."

The subject was closed. Oliver said, "Your brother and I had a talk when he was having a bath. You're Jody and Caroline Cliburn."

"Yes."

"And I'm Oliver Cairney. Did he tell you?"

"Yes, he did. He just did."

"You've come from London?"

"Yes."

"And you ditched the car at the bottom of my drive."

"Yes."

"And you were heading for Strathcorrie?"

"Yes. Our brother works there. In the hotel."

"And he's expecting you?"

"We sent him a telegram. He'll be wondering what's happened to us."

Oliver looked at his watch. "It's nearly midnight. But if you like I can try and get through on the telephone. There may be a night porter on duty."

She looked grateful. "Oh, would you do that?"

"I can always try." But the telephone was dead. "The lines must be down. It's the storm."

"But what shall we do?"

"There's nothing you can do except stay here."

"But Angus . . ."

"As I said to Jody, he'll realize what's happened."

"And tomorrow?"

"If the road isn't blocked we can get to Strathcorrie by some means or other. I've a Land-Rover if the worse comes to the worst."

"And if the road is blocked?"

"Let's worry about that when it happens."

"The thing is . . . well, we haven't got an awful lot of time. We're meant to be back in London on Friday."

Oliver looked down at his drink, gently rocking the glass in his hand. "Is there anyone in London we should get in touch with? Let them know that you are safe?"

Jody looked at his sister. After a little she said, "But there's no telephone."

"But when we do have a telephone?"

She said, "No. We don't have to get in touch with anyone."

He was sure she was lying. He watched her face, saw the high cheekbones, the short blunt nose, the wide mouth. She had dark smudges beneath her eyes, and her hair was very long, pale, straight as silk. For an instant her eyes met his, and then she turned away. Oliver decided not to pursue the subject. "I only wondered," he said, mildly.

In the morning, when Caroline awoke, the snow light was reflected on the white ceiling of the big bedroom. She lay, drowsy, pillowed in goose-down and linen; heard a dog bark, and presently the grinding sound of an approaching tractor. She reached for her watch and saw that it was already past nine o'clock. She got out of bed and padded to the window and drew back the pink curtains, and was assailed by a blast of light so blinding that she blinked.

The world was white. The sky clear, and blue as a robin's egg. Long shadows lay like bruises on the sparkling ground, everything was softened and rounded by the snow. It lay along the branches of pines, and piled in white hats on the top of fence posts. Caroline threw open the window and leaned out and the air was cold and fragrant and stimulating as iced wine.

Remembering the horrors of the night before, she tried to get her bearings. In front of the house was a large open space, probably a lawn, ringed by the driveway. She saw the tall avenue up which she and Jody had struggled, leading away, down over the crest of a hill. In the distance, between folds of sloping pastures, the main road wound between dry stone walls. A car was moving, very slowly.

The tractor she had heard was coming up the avenue. As she watched, it appeared from behind a huge clump of rhododendrons, and churned carefully around the perimeter of the lawn and so out of sight behind the house.

It was too cold to be out. She drew back into her bedroom and shut the window. She thought of Jody and went to open the door that led into his room. Inside, it was dark and quiet, only his breathing stirred the silence. He was still fast asleep. She closed the door, and looked for something to put on. But there was only the sweater and the borrowed dressing-gown, so wearing these, but barefoot, she went out of the bedroom and down the passage in the hope of finding someone to help her.

She realized then that it was an enormous house. The passage came out on to a great landing, furnished with carpets and a walnut tallboy, and chairs and a table where someone had laid down a pile of clean shirts, neatly ironed. At the top of the stair, she listened and discerned distant voices. She went downstairs, and following the murmur of voices, found herself at the door of what was presumably the kitchen. She put her hands against the door and pushed, and it swung open and immediately the two people inside stopped talking, and turned to see who it was.

Oliver Cairney, in a thick cream coloured sweater, sat at the kitchen table with a mug of tea in his hand. He had been talking to the woman who stood, peeling potatoes at the sink. Middle-aged, she was, grey-haired, and with her sleeves rolled up, and a flowered pinafore tied in a bow at the back of her waist. The kitchen was warm and smelled of baking bread. Caroline felt like an intruder. She said, "I'm sorry . . ."

Oliver, who had been momentarily surprised into inactivity, put down the mug and got to his feet.

"Nothing to be sorry about. I thought you'd sleep till lunchtime."

"Jody's still asleep."

"This is Mrs Cooper. Mrs Cooper, this is Caroline Cliburn. I've just been telling Mrs Cooper what happened to you."

Mrs Cooper said, "It was a terrible night and no mistake. All the telephone lines are down."

Caroline looked at Oliver. "You mean we still can't get through?"

"No, and won't be able to for some time. Come and have a cup of tea. Come and have some breakfast. What would you like? Bacon and egg?"

But she didn't want anything. "Some tea, that would be lovely." He pulled out a chair for her and she sat at the scrubbed table. "And are we snowed up?"

"Partially. The Strathcorrie road's blocked, but we can get down to Relkirk."

Caroline's heart sank. "And . . . the car?" She was almost frightened to ask.

"Cooper's been down on the tractor to investigate."

"Is it a red tractor?"

"Yes."

"I saw it coming back up the road."

"In that case, he'll be here any moment to let us know what's going on." He had found a cup and saucer, and now poured Caroline a cup of tea from the brown teapot which sat, stewing happily, on the Aga. It was very strong, but also very hot and she drank it gratefully. She said, "I can't find my clothes."

"That'll be me," said Mrs Cooper. "I put them to dry in the hot cupboard. They should be ready by now. But, my word—" she shook her head—"you two must have got a drenching."

"They did," said Oliver. "They were like drowned rats."

By the time Caroline was dressed and downstairs again, the party had been joined by Mr Cooper, with news of the ditched car. He was a country man and his accent so strong that Caroline had difficulty in understanding what he said.

"Oh, aye, we'll get it oot o' the ditch richt enough, but there'll be no life in the engine."

"Why not?"

"Frozen stiff, I wouldna be surprised."

Oliver looked at Caroline. "Didn't you have any antifreeze?"

Caroline looked blank.

"Anti-freeze," he said again. "It doesn't mean anything to you?"

She shook her head and he turned back to Cooper. "You're quite right. Frozen stiff."

"*Should* I have had anti-freeze?"

"Well, it's a good idea."

"I didn't know. You see, it isn't my car."

"Perhaps you stole it?"

Mrs Cooper made a small sound of disapproval, a drawing-in of the breath between pursed lips. Caroline was not sure whether the disapproval was aimed at Oliver or herself. She said, with dignity, "No, of course not. We were lent it."

"I see. Well begged, borrowed, or stolen, I suggest we go down and see what can be done with it."

"Well," said Cooper, putting his old bonnet back on his head with a large red hand, and heading for the door, "If you take the Land-Rover, I'll go and find a tow-rope and maybe young Geordie to give me a hand, and we'll see if we can get it out with the tractor."

When he had gone, Oliver looked at Caroline. "Are you coming?"

"Yes."

"You'll need boots."

"I haven't got any."

"There are some here . . ."

She followed him into an old wash-house, now used as a catch-all for raincoats, rubber boots, dog-baskets, a rusty bicycle or two and a brand-new washing machine. After some searching, Oliver produced a pair of rubber boots which more or less fitted and a black oilskin coat. Caroline put this on and flipped her hair free of the collar, and then, suitably attired, followed him out into the glittering morning.

"Winter snow, spring sun," said Oliver, with satisfaction as they trod across the pristine snow towards the closed doors of the garage.

"Will the snow last?"

"Probably not. Though it'll take a bit of melting. Nine inches fell last night."

"It was spring in London."

"That's what your brother said."

He reached up to unsnib bolts, and opened the wide double doors of the garage. Inside were two cars, the dark green sports saloon and the Land-Rover. "We'll take the Land-Rover," he said, "and then we won't get stuck."

Caroline climbed in. They backed out of the garage, drove around the house and down the avenue, cautiously following the dark tracks that Mr Cooper's tractor had already made. The morning was completely quiet, all sound muffled by the snow, and yet there was life about . . . here tracks ran beneath the trees, and the small starred footprints of random birds. High above, the branches of the beeches met in a soaring arch, a lace-like tangle silhouetted against the pale, bright morning sky.

They came out through the gate, and on to the road and into blinding sunshine. Oliver stopped the Land-Rover by the verge and they both got out. Caroline saw now the hump-backed bridge which had been their downfall, and the disconsolate shape of Caleb's car, muffled in snow, all askew in the ditch, the ground about it patterned with Mr Cooper's large-booted footprints. It looked finished, mummified, as though it would never move again. Caroline felt dreadfully guilty.

Oliver got the door open and with care inserted half of himself into the driving-seat, leaving one long leg outside. He turned the key which Caroline had carelessly left in the ignition and there was an agonized sound from the engine and a strong smell of burning. Without saying a word, he got out of the car again and slammed the door shut. "Hopeless," she heard him mutter, and felt not only guilty but a fool as well.

She said, with some vague notion of defending herself, "I didn't know about the anti-freeze. I told you it wasn't my car."

He made no reply to this, but went around the car, kicking the snow from the back tyres, then crouching on the snowy road to see if the back axle had become wedged against the edge of the ditch.

She found this all very depressing, and all at once, felt near tears. Everything was going wrong. She and Jody were stuck here, with this unsympathetic man. Caleb's car was useless, there were no telephones to Strathcorrie and the road was blocked. Blinking back tears, she turned to look up the road, which wound on, up and over the crest of a small hill. The snow lay thick and white between the dry stone dykes, a breeze moved, a baby sister of the gale last night, and blew a soft drift of snow, like smoke, off the fields and on to the drifts which were already piled, like glistening sculptures, in the angles of the dykes. Somewhere in the still morning, a curlew dropped from the sky, calling his long liquid cry. And then the air was motionless again.

Behind her, Oliver's footsteps squeaked across the snow. She turned to face him, hands buried deep in the pockets of the borrowed oilskin.

"It's had it, I'm afraid," he told her.

Caroline was horrified. "But can't it be mended?"

"Oh, yes. Cooper'll get it out with the tractor, and along to the garage down the road. He's a good man there. The Mini'll be ready for you tomorrow, or maybe the day after." Something in her face made him add, as though trying to bolster her spirits, "Even if you had a car, you can see you'd never be able to drive it to Strathcorrie. The road's impassable."

She turned again to look. "But when do you think it'll be clear?"

"As soon as the snow-plough gets around to it. A fall like this, at the very tail end of the winter, is inclined to disrupt everything. We just have to be patient."

He opened the door of the Land-Rover for her, and stood, waiting for her to get in. Slowly, Caroline did so. He shut the door and came around and got in behind the wheel. She thought that he would drive her back to the house, but instead he lit a cigarette, and sat smoking it, apparently deep in thought.

Caroline felt apprehensive. Cars were good places to be with a person you liked. But not good if the person was going to ask a lot of questions you didn't feel like answering.

And the moment he spoke, her fears were justified.

"When did you say you had to be back in London?"

"Friday. That's when I *said* we'd be back."

"Who did you say it to?"

". . . Caleb. The man who lent us the car."

"What about your parents."

"Our parents are dead."

"Isn't there anyone? There must be someone. I can't believe the pair of you keep house together, on your own." Despite himself, Oliver grinned at the thought. "The situation would be fraught with the most appalling disasters."

Caroline did not think this was particularly funny. She said, coldly, "If you must know, we live with my stepmother."

Oliver looked knowing. *"I see."*

"What do you see?"

"A wicked stepmother."

"She's not wicked at all. She's very nice."

"But she doesn't know where you are?"

". . . yes," said Caroline, hardly hesitating over the half-truth. And then, more convincingly, "Yes, she does. She knows we're in Scotland."

"Does she know why? About brother Angus?"

"Yes. She knows that too."

"And . . . coming all this way to find Angus. Was that for any particular reason or just to say hallo?"

"Not entirely."

"That's not an answer."

"Isn't it?"

This was followed by a long pause. After a little Oliver said, with deceptive mildness, "You know, I have the strongest feeling that I'm skating on very thin ice. I think you should know that I don't give a damn about what you're up to, but I do feel, very slightly, that I should be responsible for your brother. After all, he's only . . . eleven?"

"I can be responsible for Jody."

His voice was quiet. "You might both have died last night. You know that, don't you?" Caroline stared at him, and saw, to her astonishment, that he meant what he said.

"But I saw the light before I left the car behind. Otherwise, we'd have stayed, and just sat the storm out."

"Blizzards are something to be reckoned with in this part of the world. You were lucky."

"And you were kind. More than kind. And I haven't thanked you properly. But I still feel that the sooner we get to Angus and out from under your feet, the better."

"We'll see how it goes. And incidentally, I have to go out today, I have a lunch appointment in Relkirk. But Mrs Cooper will feed you and Jody, and by the time I'm back, perhaps the Strathcorrie road will be open and I can drive you both up and deliver you to your brother."

Caroline considered this, and found that for some reason, the idea of Oliver Cairney and Angus Cliburn meeting, was not a good one.

"Surely there's some way I could . . ."

"No." Oliver leaned forward and stubbed out his cigarette. "No, there is no other way of getting to Strathcorrie, short of flying. So you just sit tight and wait for me at Cairney. Understood?"

Caroline opened her mouth to argue, caught his eye, and shut her mouth again. She nodded reluctantly. "All right."

For a moment she thought he was going to continue the discussion, but his attention was mercifully diverted by the arrival of the tractor, with Mr Cooper at the wheel and a young boy in a knitted hat, perched up on the seat behind him. Oliver got out of the Land-Rover and went to assist them; but it was a tedious business, and by the time Caleb's car had been swept clear of snow, grit shovelled beneath its wheels, ropes attached to the back axle and two or three abortive attempts made to drag it clear before it finally, protestingly came, it was nearly eleven o'clock. Caroline watched the small cavalcade set off in the direction of the garage, Cooper at the wheel of the tractor, and Geordie in the Mini, steering an unsteady course at the end of the tow rope. She felt terrible.

"I do hope it will be all right," she told Oliver as he climbed back beside her. "It wouldn't be so bad if it were my car, but I promised Caleb I'd take such care of it."

"It wasn't your fault. It could have happened to anybody. By the time the garage have finished with it, it'll probably be better than ever." He looked at his watch. "We must move, I've got to get changed and into Relkirk by twelve-thirty."

They returned to the house in silence, parked at the door and went indoors. At the foot of the stairs Oliver stopped and looked at Caroline.

"You'll be all right?"

"Of course."

"I'll see you later then."

Caroline watched him go upstairs, his long legs taking the stairs two at a time. Then she shed herself of the oilskin and the large boots and went in search of Jody. The kitchen was empty, but she found Mrs Cooper vacuuming the enormous turkey-carpeted wastes of a little-used dining-room. She switched off the machine when Caroline appeared at the door.

"Did you get your motor sorted?" she asked.

"Yes. Your husband's very kindly taken it to the garage. Have you seen Jody?"

"Yes, he's up and about, the dear wee soul. Came downstairs, and had his breakfast with me in the kitchen, right as rain. Two boiled eggs he had and toast and honey and a glass of milk. Then I showed him the boys' old nursery and he's there now, up to high doh with all the bricks and cars and goodness knows what."

"Where is the nursery?"

"Come away and I'll show you."

She abandoned her cleaning and led the way up a small back staircase and through a door into a white-painted, blue-carpeted passage. "This was the nursery wing in the old days, the children had it all to themselves. It's not used now, of course, hasn't been for years, but I lit a wee fire, so it's nice and warm." She opened a door and stood aside for Caroline to go in. It was a big room, with a bay window looking out over the garden. A fire burned behind a tall fender, there were old armchairs and a sagging couch, bookshelves, an ancient tailless rocking horse, and on the floor, in the middle of the threadbare carpet, Jody, surrounded by a fortification of wooden bricks which spread to the corners of the room, all set about with model cars, toy soldiers, cowboys, knights-in-armour and farmyard animals. He looked up as she came in, his concentration so intent that he didn't even look embarrassed at being caught in such a babyish occupation.

"Heavens," said Caroline. "How long has it taken you to build this lot?"

"Since breakfast. Don't knock that tower over."

"I wasn't going to." She stepped carefully over it and made for the fireplace where she stood, leaning against the fender.

Mrs Cooper was full of admiration. "I've never seen anything so neat! And all the wee roads! You must have used up every brick in the place."

"I have, just about." Jody smiled at her. They were obviously already the best of friends.

"Well, I'll leave you then. And lunch is at half past twelve. Apple pie I've made and there's a wee bit of cream. Do you like apple pie. pet?"

"Yes, I love it."

"That's good." She went away. They heard her humming to herself. "Isn't she nice?" said Jody, aligning two tall bricks to make a ceremonial gateway into his fort.

"Yes, isn't she? Did you sleep all right?"

"Yes, for hours. It's a super house." He piled on another couple of bricks to make a really high gateway.

"The car's gone to the garage. Mr Cooper took it. It didn't have any anti-freeze."

"Silly old Caleb," said Jody. He chose an arched brick and placed it carefully, crowning his masterpiece. He put his cheek to the carpet, looking through the archway, thinking himself tiny, pretending that he would be able to ride through it on a great white charger, with the plume on his helmet fluttering in the breeze and his quartered banner held high.

"Jody, last night, when you were talking in your bath, you didn't say anything about Angus, did you? To Oliver Cairney?"

"No. Just that we were going to find him."

"Or about Diana? Or Hugh?"

"He never asked."

"Don't say anything."

Jody looked up. "How much longer are we going to stay here?"

"Oh, no time. We'll find Angus this afternoon, we'll go to Strathcorrie when the roads have been cleared."

Jody made no comment on this. She watched him take a little horse from an open box, then search for the knight that would fit into its saddle. He selected one, fitted the two together, held them off for a moment to gauge the effect. He placed the rider, with the utmost precision, beneath his archway.

He said, "Mrs Cooper told me something."

"What did she tell you?"

"This isn't his house."

"What do you mean, it isn't his house? It has to be his house."

"It belonged to his brother. Oliver lives in London, but his brother used to live here. He used to farm. That's why there are dogs and tractors and things about the place."

"What happened to his brother?"

"He was killed," said Jody. "In a car crash. Last week."

Killed in a car crash. Something, some memory, stirred in the back of Caroline's subconscious, but was almost at once lost in horror, as the implication of Jody's cool statement made itself felt. She found that she had put a hand over her mouth as though to choke back the world. Killed.

"That's why Oliver's here." Jody's voice was off-hand, a sure sign that he was distressed. "For the funeral and everything. To tie things up, Mrs Cooper says. He's going to sell this house and the farm and everything and never come back." He stood up carefully, trod his way over to Caroline's side, and stood close, and she knew that for all his apparent coolness, he was, all at once, in need of comfort.

She put her arm around him. She said, "And in the middle of it all, we had to turn up. Poor man."

"Mrs Cooper says it was a good thing. She says it keeps his mind off his sorrow." He looked up at her. "When will we get to Angus?"

"Today," Caroline promised him without any hesitation. "Today."

Besides the apple pie and cream, there was mince for lunch, baked potatoes and mashed swedes. "Chappit neeps" Mrs Cooper called them, ladling them on to Jody's plate. Caroline, who had thought she was hungry, discovered that she was not, but Jody ate his way through the lot and then attacked with relish a bar of home-made "taiblet."

"And now, what are you ones going to do with yourselves for the rest of the day? Mr Cairney won't be back till tea-time."

"Can I go on playing in the nursery?" Jody wanted to know.

"Of course, pet." Mrs Cooper looked at Caroline.

Caroline said, "I shall go for a walk."

Mrs Cooper seemed surprised. "Have you not had enough fresh air for one day?"

"I like being out. And it's so pretty with the snow."

"It's clouding over now, though, it won't be such a fine afternoon."

"I don't mind."

Jody was torn. "Do you *mind* if I don't come with you?"

"Of course not."

"I rather thought I might build a grandstand. You know, to watch the jousting."

"You do that."

Taken up with his plans, Jody excused himself and disappeared upstairs to put them into action. Caroline offered to help Mrs Cooper with the dishes but was told no, away out with you, before the rain comes on. So she went out of the kitchen and across the hall, put on the oilskin and the rubber boots she had worn that morning, tied a scarf around her head and let herself out of the house.

Mrs Cooper had been right about the day. Clouds had rolled in from the west, there was a mildness in the air, the sun had disappeared. She drove her hands deep into the pockets of the coat and set off, across the lawn, down the avenue, and through the gates on to the road. She turned left, in the direction of Strathcorrie, and started to walk.

You sit tight and wait for me at Cairney, Oliver had said, and if she wasn't there by the time he returned he would probably be furious, but taking the long view, Caroline could not see that this would matter very much. After today, they would probably never see him again. She would write, of course, to thank him for his kindness. But she would never see him again.

And, somehow, it was important that when she and Angus met up once more, after all these years, they did not do so beneath the eyes of some critical stranger. The worst thing about Angus was that you could never depend on him. He had always been the most unpredictable person in the world, vague, elusive and utterly maddening. From the very beginning she had had reservations about this wild scheme of coming to Scotland to find him, but somehow Jody's enthusiasm had been infectious. He was so sure that Angus would be waiting for them, delighted to see them, anxious to help, that, from the safe distance of London, he had managed to convince Caroline as well.

But now, in the chill light of a Scottish afternoon, her doubts returned. Angus would of course *be* at the Strathcorrie Hotel because that was where he was working, but the fact that he cleaned shoes and carried logs was no insurance that he would not have long hair, a beard, bare feet and no intention whatsoever of doing anything to help his brother and sister. She imagined Oliver Cairney's reaction to such an attitude and knew that she could not have borne him to be present to witness the great reunion.

Besides, there was the new knowledge of his brother's recent death, and a sensation of the most acute embarrassment that they had encroached on Oliver's kindness and taken advantage of his unquestioning hospitality at such a totally inopportune time. There was no doubt that the sooner he was shed of them the better. There was no doubt that coming to find Angus now, on her own, was the only possible course to take.

Trudging down the long, snow-packed road, she filled the time convincing herself that this was really so.

She had been walking for over an hour, without any idea of how many miles she had covered, when a lorry overtook her, slowly grinding up the slope behind her. It was the County snow-plough, its huge steel plough cutting through the snow like the bows of a ship through water, sending out a spuming wake of slush on either side of the road.

Caroline got out of the way, clambering up on to the top of the wall, but the snow-plough stopped, and the man inside opened the door and called down to her.

"Where are you going?"

"Strathcorrie."

"That's another six miles. Do you want a ride?"

"Yes, please."

"Come away then." She scrambled down off the wall, and he put down a horny hand and helped her up, moving across to make space for her. His mate, a much older man driving the lorry, said dourly, "I hope you're no' in a hurry. The snow's lying deep on the brow of the hill."

"I'm in no hurry. Just so that I don't have to walk."

"Aye, it's durrty weather."

He crashed the heavy gears, threw off the handbrake, and they moved on, but it was, in truth, a slow progress. At intervals the two men got down and did a bit of strenuous shoveling, clearing the grit piles that had been left, strategically, at the sides of the road. Damp oozed its way through the windows of the cab, and Caroline's feet, in her ill-fitting boots, became like two lumps of ice.

But at last they crested the final hill and the kindly roadman said, "There's Strathcorrie now," and she saw the white and grey country-side drop before them, into a deep glen, and a long meandering loch, quite still, and steel-grey with reflected sky.

On the far side of the water the hills climbed again, patterned black with stands of fir and pine, and beyond their gentle summits could be seen other peaks, a range of distant, northern mountains. And directly below, clustered around the narrow end of the loch, lay the village. She saw the church and little streets of grey houses, and there was a small boat yard, with jetties and moorings and small craft pulled up on the shingle for the winter.

"What a pretty place!" said Caroline.

"Aye," said the roadman. "And they get a gey lot of visitors in the summer months. Sailing boats for hire, bed and breakfast, cara-vans . . ."

The road ran downhill. The snow here, for some reason, lay not so thick and they were making better time. "Where do you want us to leave you?" the driver asked.

"The hotel. The Strathcorrie Hotel. Do you know where that is?"

"Oh, aye, I ken it fine."

In the village, the grey streets were wet, snow melting in the gutters, dropping, with soft plopping sounds, from sloping eaves. The snow-plough drove down the main street, passed under an ornamental Gothic archway, built to commemorate some long-forgotten Victorian occasion, and came to a halt before a long white-washed building, fronted by a cobbled pavement and with a sign swinging over the door. *Strathcorrie Hotel. Visitors Welcome.*

There was no sign of life. "Is it open?" Caroline asked doubtfully.

"Aye, it's open right enough. It's just no' very busy."

She thanked them for their kindness and climbed down from the snow-plough. As it moved away, she crossed the road, and the cobbled pavement, and went in through the revolving door. Inside it smelled of stale cigarette smoke and boiled cabbage. There was a sad picture of a roe deer on a wet hill, and a desk with a notice, *Reception,* but no one to do any receiving. There was, however, a bell, which Caroline rang. In a moment a woman appeared from an office. She wore a black dress and spectacles trimmed with diamanté, and did not look too pleased at being interrupted in the middle of the afternoon, especially by a girl in jeans and an oilskin with a red cotton handkerchief tied around her head.

"Yes?"

"I'm so sorry to bother you, but I wondered if I could speak to Angus Cliburn."

"Oh," said the woman immediately. "Angus isn't here." She looked quite pleased to be able to impart this information.

Caroline simply stared at her. Overhead a clock ticked sonorously. Somewhere, in the back regions of the hotel, a man started to sing. The woman re-adjusted her spectacles.

"He *was* here, of course," she enlarged, as though conceding a point to Caroline. She hesitated and then said, "Did you by any chance send him a telegram? There is a telegram for him, but of course he'd gone by the time it arrived." She opened a drawer and took out the orange envelope. "I had to open it, you see, and I'd have let you know he wasn't here, only there wasn't any address."

"No, of course . . ."

"He was here, mind you. He worked here for a month or more. Helping out. We were a little short-staffed, you see."

"But where is he now?"

"Oh, I couldn't say. He went with an American lady, driving her car for her. She was staying here, and hadn't anyone to drive her, so as we had a replacement for Angus by then, we let him go. A chauffeur," she added as though Caroline would never have heard of the word.

"But when are they coming back?"

"Oh, in a day or so. The end of the week Mrs Mcdonald said."

"Mrs Mcdonald?"

"Yes, the American lady. Her husband's ancestors came from this part of Scotland. That's why she was so keen to go sight-seeing, hired the car and got Angus to drive her."

Back at the end of the week. That meant Friday, or Saturday. But Caroline and Jody had to be back in London by Friday. She couldn't wait until the week-end. She was getting married on Tuesday. On Tuesday she was getting married to Hugh, and she had to be there, because there was a wedding rehearsal on Monday, and Diana would be frantic, and all the presents.

Her thoughts galloped uselessly, to and fro, like a distracted runaway horse. She pulled herself up and told herself that she must be practical. And then realized that she could not think of one practical thing to say or to do. *I am at the end of my tether.* This was how it felt. Now, when people said *I am at the end of my tether,* she, Caroline, would understand.

The woman behind the desk was becoming a little impatient with all this waiting about. "Did you particularly want to see Angus?"

"Yes. I'm his sister. It's rather important."

"Where did you come from today?"

Without thought Caroline told her. "From Cairney."

"But that's eight miles. And the road's blocked."

"I walked a bit, and then I got a lift with the snow-plough."

They would have to wait for Angus. Perhaps they could stay here, at the hotel. She wished she had brought Jody with her.

"Would you have two rooms vacant that we could have?"

"We?"

"I have another brother. He's not with me just now."

The woman looked doubtful, but she said "Just a moment" and went back to her office to consult some book. Caroline leaned against the counter and decided that it was no good getting into a panic, it only made you feel ill. It made you feel sick.

And then she knew it was back again, the old nausea, the knife-like pain in her stomach. It had taken her completely by surprise, like some horrible monster waiting around the corner to pounce. She tried to ignore it, but it was not to be ignored. It grew, with frightening speed, like a huge balloon being pumped up with air. Enormous, and so intensely agonizing that it left no room in her consciousness for anything else. She was made of pain, pain stretched to the most distant horizon, she closed her eyes and there came a sound like the screaming of a distant alarm bell.

And then, when she thought she could bear it no longer, it began to die away, slipping down and off her, like some discarded garment.

After a little, she opened her eyes, and found herself looking straight into the horrified face of the receptionist. She wondered how long she had been standing there.

"Are you all right?"

"Yes." She tried to smile. Her face was wet with sweat. "Indigestion, I think. I've had it before. And then the walk . . ."

"I'll get you a glass of water. You'd better sit down."

"I'm all right."

But something was wrong with the woman's face; in a strange blur it was approaching and receding. She was speaking, Caroline could see her mouth open and shut, but she made no sound. Caroline put out a hand and took hold of the edge of the counter, but it did no good, and the last thing she remembered was the brightly patterned carpet swinging up to hit her with a resounding clout on the side of the head.

5

Oliver did not get back to Cairney until half past four. He was tired. Duncan Fraser, besides standing him a heavy luncheon, had insisted on discussing every aspect of the financial and legal details of the taking over of Cairney. Nothing had been left out and Oliver's head swam with facts and figures. Acreages, yields, heads of cattle, the value of cottages, the condition of steadings and barns. It was necessary, of course, and right, but he had found it distressing, and he made the long drive home through the darkening afternoon in a state of black depression, trying to accept the truth; that, by giving up Cairney, even to Duncan, it was inevitable that he was giving up something of himself, and cutting away the last of the connections that held him to his youth.

The conflict within himself had left him drained of energy. His head ached, and he could think of nothing but the sanctuary of his home, the comfort of his own armchair, his own fireside, and possibly, a soothing cup of tea.

The house had never looked so secure, so welcoming. He took the Land-Rover around to the garage, parked it there, and went indoors, through the kitchen. He found Mrs Cooper, at her ironing board, but with her eyes on the door. When he appeared, she gave a sigh of relief, and set the iron down with a thump.

"Oh, Oliver, I hoped it was you. I heard the car, and I hoped it was you."

Something in her face made him say, "What's wrong?"

"It's just the boy's sister went out for a walk, and she's not back yet, and it's nearly dark."

Oliver stood there, in his overcoat, and slowly digested this unwelcome piece of information.

"When did she go?"

"After lunch. Not that she ate anything, just picked away, didn't take enough to keep a flea alive."

"But it's . . . half past four."

"That's just it."

"Where's Jody?"

"He's in the nursery. He's fine and not worried. I took him his tea, the wee lamb."

Oliver frowned. "But where did she go?"

"She didn't say. 'I'm just going for a wee walk,' she said." Mrs Cooper's face was drawn with anxiety. "You don't think something could have happened?"

"I shouldn't be surprised," said Oliver, bitterly. "She's such a fool, she could drown herself in a puddle."

"Oh, poor wee soul . . ."

"Poor wee soul nothing, she's a bloody nuisance," said Oliver brutally.

He was headed for the back staircase, meaning to go and find Jody and pick his brains, but at that moment the telephone started ringing. Oliver's first reactions were that at last the lines had been repaired, but Mrs Cooper slapped her hand over her heart and said, "Perhaps that's the po-lice now."

"Probably nothing of the sort," said Oliver, but for all that he went, more swiftly than usual, out of the kitchen and along to the library to answer the call.

"Cairney," he barked.

"Is that Cairney House?" A female voice, very refined.

"Yes it is, Oliver Cairney speaking."

"Oh, Mr Cairney, this is Mrs Henderson speaking from the Strathcorrie Hotel."

Oliver braced himself. "Yes?"

"There's a young lady here, she came to inquire for her brother, who used to work here . . ."

Used to work? "Yes?"

"She said she'd been staying at Cairney."

"That's right."

"Well, I think perhaps you should come and fetch her, Mr Cairney. She doesn't seem to be at all well, and she fainted and then she was very . . . sick." She brought the word out reluctantly as though it were rude.

"How did she get to Strathcorrie?"

"She walked part of the way she said, and then she got a lift with the snow-plough."

That meant that at least the road would be open. "And where is she now?"

"I put her to lie down . . . she seemed so unwell."

"Does she know you've called me?"

"No. I thought better not to say."

"Don't say. Don't say anything. Just keep her there till I come."

"Yes, Mr Cairney. And I'm so sorry."

"Not at all. You were quite right to call. We were worried. Thank you. I'll be there as soon as I can."

Caroline was asleep when he came. No, not asleep, but suspended in that delicious state between sleeping and waking; warm, and comforted by the touch of blankets. Until the sound of his deep voice cut through her drowsiness like a knife and she was instantly wide awake, alert and clear-headed. She remembered saying that she had come from Cairney and cursed her own careless tongue. But the pain was gone, and the sleep refreshed her, so when, without so much as a cursory knock, Oliver Cairney threw open her door and marched in, Caroline was ready for him, with all her defences up.

"Oh, what a shame, you've come all this way, and there's really nothing wrong at all. Look." She sat up. "I'm perfectly all right." He wore a grey overcoat and a black tie and this reminded her of his brother and she went on in a rush. "It's just that it was rather a long walk, at least it wasn't all that long because I got a lift from the snow-plough." He slammed the door shut and came to lean against the brass rail at the end of the bed. "Did you bring Jody?" she asked brightly. "Because we can stay here. They've got rooms, and we'd be better to wait here till Angus gets back. He's away you see, just for another couple of days, with an American lady . . ."

Oliver said, "Shut up."

No one had ever spoken to Caroline in that voice before and she was utterly silenced. "I told you to stay at Cairney. To wait."

"I couldn't."

"Why not?"

"Because Jody told me about your brother. Mrs Cooper told Jody. And it was so terrible us turning up, just then. I was so sorry . . . I didn't know . . ."

"How could you know?"

". . . but at such a time."

"It makes no difference one way or the other," said Oliver bluntly. "How do you feel now?"

"I'm perfectly all right."

"You fainted." It sounded like an accusation.

"So silly, I never faint."

"The trouble is, you never eat anything. If you choose to be so moronic you deserve to faint. Now get your coat on and I'll take you home."

"But I told you, we can stay here. We'll wait for Angus here."

"You can wait for Angus at Cairney." He went over to the chair and picked up the black oilskin.

Caroline frowned. She said, "Suppose I don't want to come? I don't have to."

"Suppose for once you do what you're told. Suppose you think about someone other than yourself? Mrs Cooper was grey in the face when I got back, imagining every sort of ghastly disaster that might have happened to you."

She felt a pang of guilt. "And Jody?"

"He's all right. I left him watching television. Now, are you coming?"

There was nothing else to do. Caroline got off the bed, let him help her into the oilskin, trod her feet into the rubber boots, and then followed him meekly downstairs.

"Mrs Henderson!"

She appeared from her office, standing behind her desk like an obliging shop-assistant.

"Oh, you found her, Mr Cairney, that's good." She lifted the flap of the counter and came out to join them. "How are you feeling, dear?" she said to Caroline.

"I'm all right." She added on an afterthought, "Thank you," although it was hard to forgive Mrs Henderson for having telephoned for Oliver.

"It was no trouble. And when Angus gets back . . ."

Oliver said, "Tell him his sister's at Cairney."

"Of course. And I'm glad you're feeling better."

Caroline made for the door. Behind her Oliver thanked Mrs Henderson once again, and then they were both out in the cold, soft, windy twilight, and she was clambering defeatedly back into the Land-Rover.

They drove in silence. The promised thaw had turned the snow to slush and the road over the hill was comparatively clear. Above, grey clouds were being bowled aside by a west wind leaving spaces of shining sky the colour of sapphires. Through the open window of the Land-Rover came the smell of turf and damp peat. Curlews rose from the margins of a small reed-fringed loch, and all at once it seemed possible that the empty trees would soon be in bud and the long-awaited spring almost upon them.

And Caroline was reminded of that evening in London, driving to Arabella's with Hugh. She remembered the city's lights reflected orange in the sky, and how she had rolled down the window and let the wind blow her hair and wished that she was in the country. It was only three–four days ago, and yet now it felt like a lifetime. As though it had happened to another girl in another time entirely.

An illusion. She was Caroline Cliburn with a hundred unsolved problems sitting on her plate. She was Caroline Cliburn and she was going to have to get back to London before all hell broke loose. She was Caroline Cliburn and she was going to marry Hugh Rashley. On Tuesday.

That was real. To make it more real she thought of the house in Milton Gardens awash with wedding presents. The white dress, hanging in her cupboard, the caterers coming in with their trestle-tables and their stiff white damask tableclothes. She thought of champagne glasses massed like soap bubbles, gardenias in a bouquet, the pop of corks and the cliché of speeches; and she thought of Hugh, considerate, organized Hugh, who had never so much as raised his voice to Caroline, let alone tell her to shut up.

This rankled still. Indignant at the memory, she let her resentments swell. Resentment at Angus, for letting her down just when she needed him most; swanning off in a car with some old American dowager, leaving no address, no date of return, nothing definite. Resentment at Mrs Henderson, with her diamanté spectacles and her air of humble efficiency, telephoning Oliver Cairney when the last thing Caroline wanted was his renewed interference. And finally resentment at Oliver himself, this overbearing man who had taken on more than could possibly be justified in the name of hospitable concern.

The Land-Rover ground its way over the crest of the hill and the road sloped away from them, leading back to Cairney. Oliver changed gear and the tyres bit deep into the slushy snow. The silence between them was thick with his disapproval. She wished that he would say something. Anything. All her resentments capsuled into an irritation that was directed solely at him. It grew until it could no longer be contained, and she said at last, frostily, "This is ridiculous."

"What is ridiculous?" His chill voice matched her own.

"The whole situation. Everything."

"I don't know enough about the situation to comment on that. In fact, apart from knowing that you and Jody appeared at Cairney out of a snow storm, I am completely in the dark."

"It isn't your business," said Caroline, sounding ruder than she had meant to.

"But what is my business is seeing that your brother doesn't have to suffer from any more of your idiocies."

"If Angus had been at Strathcorrie . . ."

He did not let her finish. "That's hypothetical. He wasn't. And I have a strange feeling that you weren't too surprised. What sort of a guy is he, anyway?" Caroline maintained what she hoped was a dignified silence. Oliver said "I see" in the smug voice of one who understands all.

"No, you don't. You don't know a thing about him. You don't even understand."

"Oh, shut up," said Oliver, unforgivably, for the second time, and Caroline turned away from him and stared out of the darkening window, so that he would neither see nor guess at the smarting prick of tears that suddenly stung her eyes.

In the dusk the house stood foursquare, yellow lights suffused from behind drawn curtains. Oliver stopped the Land-Rover at the door and got out, and slowly, reluctantly, Caroline climbed down too, and followed him up the steps and passed him as she stood aside, holding the door open, letting her go ahead. Feeling like a naughty child, brought to book, she would not even look at him. The door slammed shut behind them, and at once, as though this sound were a signal, there came the sound of Jody's voice. A door opened, his footsteps came up the passage from the kitchen. He appeared at a run, then stopped dead when he saw that only two people stood there. His eyes went to the door behind Caroline and then back to her face. He was very still.

"Angus?" he said.

He had been expecting her to bring Angus back with her. She said, hating having to tell him, "Angus wasn't there."

There was a silence. Then Jody said casually, "You didn't find him."

"He's been there, working there. But he's gone away for a few days." She went on, trying to sound confident. "He'll be back. In a day or so. There's nothing to worry about."

"But Mrs Cooper said you were ill."

"I'm not," said Caroline quickly.

"But she said . . ."

Oliver interrupted. "All that's wrong with your sister is that she never does what she's told and she never eats anything." He sounded thoroughly put out. Jody watched as he unbuttoned his tweed over-coat and slung it over the end of the banister. "Where's Mrs Cooper?"

"In the kitchen."

"Go and tell her everything's all right. I've brought Caroline back and she's going to bed and to have some supper and tomorrow she'll be as right as rain." And when Jody still hesitated, Oliver went over and turned him and gave him a gentle shove in the direction from whence he had appeared. "Go on. There's nothing to worry about. I promise you."

Jody departed. The kitchen door swung shut, distantly, they heard his voice, relaying the message. Oliver turned to Caroline.

"And now," he said with deceptive pleasantness, "you are going upstairs to bed, and Mrs Cooper will bring you some supper on a tray. It's as simple as that."

The tone of his voice kindled an old, rare stubbornness. A stubbornness that had, from time to time, won Caroline her own way in childhood; had finally broken down her stepmother's objections to the Drama School. Hugh, perhaps, had early recognized this streak in her character, for his handling of her had always been tactful to a degree, coaxing, suggesting, leading her by a string when she would have refused to be driven.

Now, she pondered on the idea of making a final terrible scene, but, as Oliver Cairney continued to stand, waiting, politely implacable, her resolution faded. Finding excuses for her surrender, she told herself that she was tired, too tired for any further arguments. And the thought of bed and warmth and privacy was suddenly very appealing. Without a word, she turned away from him and went upstairs, a step at a time, her hand running the length of the long, polished banister rail.

When she had gone Oliver made his way back to the kitchen where he found Mrs Cooper preparing supper and Jody at the scrubbed table, struggling with an elderly jigsaw which, when completed, would be a picture of an old-fashioned steam engine. Oliver remembered the jigsaw, remembered doing it with his mother and Charles to help. Whiling away long wet afternoons, waiting for the rain to stop so that they could get out of doors again to play.

He leaned over Jody's shoulder. "You're doing very well," he told him.

"I can't find that bit. With the sky and the bit of branch. If I could find that bit, I could join this other chunk up."

Oliver started to search for the elusive piece. From the stove Mrs Cooper said, "Is the young lady all right?"

Oliver did not look up. "Yes, she's all right. She's gone to bed."

"What happened to her?" Jody asked.

"She fainted and then she was sick."

"I hate being sick."

Oliver grinned. "So do I."

"I'm sieving a nice wee bowl of broth," said Mrs Cooper. "When you're not well, the last thing, you want is a supper that lies heavy on your stomach."

Oliver agreed that indeed you didn't. He ran the missing piece of the jigsaw to earth and handed it to Jody.

"How's that?"

"That's it." Jody was delighted at Oliver's cleverness. "Oh, thank you, I've been looking and looking at that bit and never even saw it was the right one." He looked up to smile. "It helps having two people to do it, doesn't it? Will you go on helping?"

"Well, right now I'm going to have a bath and then I'm going to have a drink, and then we'll have supper together, you and I. But after supper, we'll see if we can finish the jigsaw."

"Was it yours?"

"Mine, or Charles's, I can't remember."

"It's a funny sort of train."

"Steam engines were splendid. They made such a magnificent noise."

"I know. I've seen them on films."

He had his bath and dressed and was on his way downstairs, headed for the library and the drink he had promised himself when he remembered, out of the blue, that he was due to dine, that very evening, at Rossie Hill. The shock of this, however, was not so great as the sense of surprise that he had forgotten the appointment at all. But, despite the fact that he had seen Duncan Fraser at lunchtime, and had even spoken of the projected dinner, the frantic events of the afternoon and evening had succeeded in driving it clean out of his head.

And now it was half past seven and he was dressed not in a dinner-suit, but in an old polo-necked sweater and a pair of washed-out corduroys. For a moment he hesitated, pulling at his lower lip, and trying to decide what to do, but his mind was finally made up by the image of Jody, who had spent a lonely and distressing afternoon, and whom Oliver had promised company for the evening, and assistance with the jigsaw puzzle. That settled it. He went along to the library, picked up the receiver and dialled the Rossie Hill number. After a moment Liz herself answered the call.

"Hallo."

"Liz."

"Oh, Oliver, are you ringing to say you'll be late? Because if so it doesn't matter, I forgot to put the pheasant in and besides . . ."

He interrupted her. "No, I didn't ring for that. I rang to call off. I can't make it."

"But . . . I . . . Father said . . ." and then in quite a different voice, "Are you all right?" She sounded as though he might suddenly have gone mad. "Not ill, or anything?"

"No. It's just that I can't make it . . . I'll explain . . ."

She said, her voice cool, "It wouldn't have anything to do with the girl and the boy you've got staying at Cairney?"

Oliver was astonished. He had said nothing to Duncan about the Cliburns, not with any intention of concealment, but simply because there had been other and more important subjects to discuss. "How did you know?"

"Oh, the old glen grapevine. Don't forget, our Mrs Douglas is Cooper's sister-in-law. You can't keep any secrets living up here, Oliver. You should know that by now."

He felt vaguely nettled, as though she were accusing him of being deceitful.

"It's no secret."

"Are they still there?"

"Yes."

"I shall have to come and investigate. It's intriguing."

He ignored the innuendo in her voice, and dropped the subject. "Do you forgive me for being so mannerless this evening, and crying off at such short notice?"

"It doesn't matter. These little things crop up from time to time. It just means all the more pheasant for Father and me. But come another night."

"If you'll ask me."

"I'm asking you now." But her voice was still crisp. "All you have to do, once your social life has sorted itself out, is to give me a ring."

"I'll do that," said Oliver.

" 'Bye, then."

"Goodbye."

But before the word was out of his mouth, she had already put down her receiver and cut him off.

She was annoyed with him and with some reason. He thought wistfully of the carefully set dinner-table, the candles, the pheasant and the wine. Dinner at Rossie Hill was never, at any time, an occasion to be sneezed at. He swore softly, hating the whole day, wishing for it to be over. He poured himself a drink, stronger than usual, added a splash of soda, poured some of it mindlessly down his throat, and then, feeling remotely comforted, went to look for Jody.

But he never got that far. Instead, in the passage he met Mrs Cooper, carrying a tray. There was a strange expression on her face, almost furtive, and when she saw him, her pace quickened so that she could get through the kitchen door before he reached her side.

"What's wrong, Mrs Cooper?"

With her back against the swing-door she stopped, looking anguished.

"She won't eat a mouthful, Oliver." He looked at the tray, then took the lid off the soup bowl. Steam rose in a fragrant cloud. "I did my best, I told her what you said, but she won't eat a mouthful. She says she's frightened of being sick again."

Oliver put the lid back on the soup bowl, the whisky glass on the tray, then took the lot from Mrs Cooper's hands.

He said, "We'll see about that."

He was tired and depressed no longer, simply marvellously angry. Exasperated beyond words. He marched upstairs, two at a time, went down the passage and burst into the Cairney guest room without so much as a knock on the door. She lay in the middle of the huge, pink-quilted double bed, pillows scattered on the floor, ringed by the small light of a pink-shaded bedside lamp.

Seeing her thus only increased his irritation. She was a bloody girl, she walked into his house, turned everything upside down, ruined his evening and finally lay in his own spare bed refusing to eat and driving everybody up the wall. He strode across the room and dumped the tray with some force down upon the bedside-table. The lamp shook slightly, his whisky danced and splashed.

She watched him flatly from the bed, her eyes enormous, her hair spread and tangled like skeins of creamy silk. Without a word he began gathering up the pillows, then pulled her into a sitting position and stuffed them behind her, as though she were a rag doll incapable of sitting up on her own.

Her expression was mutinous, her underlip swollen as a spoiled child's. He picked the napkin off the tray and tied it around her neck as though he had intentions of throttling her. He took the lid off the soup bowl.

She said, clearly, "If you make me eat that, I shall be sick."

Oliver reached for the spoon. "And if you are sick I shall beat you."

The lower lip trembled at the injustice of such a threat. "Now, or when I'm well again?" she inquired bitterly.

"Both," said Oliver brutally. "Now open your mouth."

When she did, more out of astonishment than anything else, he poured in the first spoonful. As she swallowed it, she gagged slightly, and sent him a look of reproachful appeal, to which he simply raised a cautionary eyebrow. The second spoonful went down. And the third. And the fourth. By now she had started to cry. Silently her eyes filled with tears, over-spilled, poured down her cheeks. Oliver ignored them, relentlessly feeding her the broth. By the time it was finished she was awash with weeping. He set down the empty bowl on the tray, and said, without sympathy, "You see, you weren't sick."

Caroline gave a great sob, incapable of comment. All at once his temper died, he wanted to smile, he was filled with a ridiculous and tender amusement. His final burst of rage, like a thunderstorm, had cleared his own personal air, and he was suddenly quite calm and relaxed, with all the troubles and frustrations of the day slotted away in their correct perspectives. All that remained was this peaceful, pretty room, the glow of the pink-shaded light, the remains of his whisky in its glass, and Caroline Cliburn, finally fed and subdued.

He pulled the napkin gently free of her neck and handed it to her. "Perhaps," he suggested, "you could use this as a handkerchief."

She sent him a grateful look and took it, wiped at cheeks, at eyes, and finally, lustily, blew her nose. A strand of hair lying close to her cheek was wet from her tears, and he put out a finger to smooth it back, away behind her ear.

It was a small, instinctive action of comfort, unpremeditated, but the unexpected physical contact sparked off a chain reaction. For an instant Caroline's face was suffused with astonishment, and then an overwhelming relief. As though it were the most natural thing in the world, she leaned forward and pressed her forehead against the rough wool of his sweater, and without thinking about it, he wrapped his arms around her thin shoulders and pulled her close, the top of her silky head tight beneath his chin. He could feel her fragility, her very bones, the beating of her heart. After a little he said, "You'll really have to tell me what it's all about, won't you?"

And Caroline nodded, thumping her head against his chest. "Yes," came her muffled voice. "I really think I will."

She started, where it had all started, on Aphros. "We went to live there after my mother died. Jody was just a baby, he could speak Greek before he spoke English. My father was an architect, he went out there to design houses, but English people started discovering Aphros and wanting to live there, and he ended up as a sort of property agent, buying houses and overseeing while they were converted and that sort of thing. Perhaps if Angus had been brought up in England he would have been different. I don't know. But we went to local schools because my father couldn't afford to send us home."

She broke off, and started trying to explain about Angus. "He'd always lived such a free life. My father never bothered about us or where we were. He knew we were safe. Angus spent most of his time with the fishermen and when he left school, he just stayed on Aphros and it never seemed to occur to anybody that he might get a job. And then Diana came."

"Your stepmother."

"Yes. She came to the island to buy a house, she came to my father to ask him to act as her agent. But she never bought the house, because she married him instead and lived with us."

"Did that make a lot of difference?"

"To Jody it did. And to me. But not to Angus. Never to Angus."

"Did you like her?"

"Yes." Caroline pleated the edge of the sheet, carefully, precisely, as though it were a finicky task directed by Diana and to be accomplished to her own exact standards. "Yes, I liked her. And so did Jody. But Angus was too old to be influenced by her and she . . . she was too wise to try to influence him. But then my father died, and she said that we must all come back to London, but Angus didn't want to come. He didn't want to stay on Aphros either. He bought a second-hand Mini Moke and he went to India, through Syria and Turkey, and we used to get postcards from him of outlandish places and nothing much else."

"But you came back to London?"

"Yes. Diana had a house in Milton Gardens. That's where we still live."

"And Angus?"

"He came there once, but it didn't work. He and Diana had a terrible row because he wouldn't conform or cut his hair or shave his beard or put on a pair of shoes. You know. And anyway, by that time

Diana had married again, an old boy-friend called Shaun Carpenter. So now she's Mrs Carpenter."

"And Mr Carpenter?"

"He's nice, but he's not a strong enough character for Diana. She gets her own way, she manipulates people, all of us, really. But in the most tactful possible way. It's hard to describe."

"And what were you doing all this time?"

"Oh, I finished school and then I went to Drama School." She looked at Oliver with the ghost of a smile. "Diana didn't want that. She was frightened I'd turn into a hippie or go on to drugs or get like Angus."

Oliver grinned. "And did you?"

"No. But she also said I wouldn't stay the course and she was right. I mean, I got through Drama School all right, and I even got a job in a Repertory theatre, but then . . ." She stopped. Oliver's face was oddly gentle, his eyes very understanding. He was easy to talk to. She had not realized how easy he would be to talk to. He had done nothing, all day, but indicate in every possible way that he thought she was a fool, but instinctively, she knew that he would not call her a fool, simply because she had fallen in love with the wrong man ". . . well, I got involved with this man. And I was stupid, I suppose, and innocent, and I thought that he wanted to go on being involved with me. But actors are single-minded creatures, and he was very career-minded and ambitious and he moved on and left me behind. He was called Drennan Colefield and he's quite famous now. You've maybe heard of him . . ."

"Yes, I have."

". . . he married a French actress. I think they live in Hollywood now. He's going to make a string of films. Anyway, after Drennan everything went wrong, and then I got pneumonia, and in the end I just gave it all up."

She began to pleat the sheet again. "And Angus?" Oliver prompted gently. "When did he turn up in Scotland?"

"Jody got a letter from him, a week or two ago. But he didn't tell about it until last Sunday night."

"And why was it so important to see him again?"

"Because of Diana and Shaun going to Canada. Shaun's got this posting to Canada, and they're going as soon as . . . well, very soon. And they're taking Jody with them. And Jody doesn't want to go, although Diana doesn't know that. But he told me and he asked me to come to Scotland with him and find Angus. He thought Angus might come to London and make a home for Jody so that Jody doesn't have to go."

"Is that likely to happen?"

Caroline said, with bleak truth, "Not particularly. But I had to try. For Jody's sake I had to try."

"Couldn't Jody stay with you?"

"No."

"Why not?"

Caroline shrugged. "It just wouldn't work out. Anyway, Diana would never agree to it. But Angus is different. Angus is twenty-five now. If Angus wanted to keep Jody, Diana couldn't stop him."

"I see."

"And so we came to find him. And we borrowed the car from Caleb Ash, he's a friend of my father's but he lives in London, in the flat at the other end of Diana's garden. He likes Diana, but I don't think he approves of the way she organizes us all and runs our lives. That's why he lent us his car, on condition we told him where we were coming."

"But you didn't tell Diana?"

"We said we were coming to Scotland. That was all. We left a letter. If we'd told her more, she'd have caught up with us long before we got here. She's that sort of person."

"Isn't she going to be very worried about you?"

"I expect so. But we said we'd be back on Friday . . ."

"But you won't. Not if Angus doesn't get back."

"I know."

"Don't you think it might be a good idea to telephone her?"

"No. Not yet. For Jody's sake, we mustn't."

"She'd understand, surely."

"In a way, but not entirely. If Angus were a different sort of person . . ." Her voice tailed hopelessly away.

"So what are we going to do?" asked Oliver.

The "we" disarmed her. She said "I don't know" but the desperate expression had gone from her face. And then, hopefully, "Wait?"

"For how long?"

"Till Friday. And then, I promise you, we'll call Diana and we'll go back to London."

Oliver considered this, and finally, with some reluctance, agreed. "Not that I approve," he added.

Caroline smiled. "That's nothing new. You've been radiating disapproval ever since we walked in through your door."

"With, you must admit, some justification."

"The only reason I went to Strathcorrie today was because of learning about your brother. I wouldn't have gone if it hadn't been for that. I felt so terrible, embarrassed, knowing we'd turned up at such a desperate time."

"It's not desperate now. It's all over."

"What are you going to do?"

"Sell Cairney and go back to London."

"Isn't that very sad?"

"Sad, but not the end of the world. Cairney, the way I remember it, is inside my head, indestructible. It's not so much the house as all the good things that happened in it. The underpinnings of a very happy life. I won't lose any of that even if I live to be an old man with white hair and no teeth."

"Like Aphros," said Caroline. "Aphros is like that for Jody and me. All the nice things that happen to me are nice because they remind me of Aphros. Sun and white houses and blue skies and winds blowing off the sea, and the smell of pine trees, and geraniums in pots. What was your brother like? Was he like you?"

"He was nice, the nicest guy in the world and he wasn't like me."

"How was he?"

"Red-headed and hard working and up to his ears in Cairney. He was a good farmer. He was a good man."

"If Angus had been like that, things would have been so different."

"If Angus had been like my brother Charles you would never have come to Scotland to look for him, never come to Cairney, and then I should never have met you both."

"That surely can't be such a good thing."

"But undoubtedly what Mrs Cooper would call an 'experience.' "

They laughed together. Their laughter was interrupted by a knock on the door, and when Caroline said "Come in," the door opened and Jody put his head around its edge.

"Jody."

He came slowly into the room. "Oliver, Mrs Cooper says to tell you supper's ready."

"Good heavens, is it that time already?" Oliver looked at his watch. "All right. I'm on my way."

Jody came to his sister's side. "Are you feeling better now?"

"Yes, much better."

Oliver stood up, picked up the empty tray and started for the door. "How's the jigsaw going?" he asked.

"I've done a bit more, but not much."

"We'll sit up all night, till it's finished." He said to Caroline, "You go to sleep now. We'll see you in the morning."

"Good night," said Jody.

"Good night, Jody."

When they had gone, she turned off the bedside lamp. Starlight shone from beyond the open window and the half-drawn curtains. A curlew called and a stirring of wind moved in the tall pines. Caroline was already on the edge of sleep, but before she finally dropped off there were two important and puzzling thoughts which occurred to her.

The first was that, after all this time, her affair with Drennan Colefield was finally over. She had talked about him, spoken his name, but the magic had gone. He was in the past now, finished and done with, and it was as though a great weight had been lifted from her shoulders. She was free again.

The second thought was even more confusing. For, although she had told Oliver everything else, she had somehow not been able to bring herself to mention Hugh. She knew that there had to be a reason for this . . . there was a reason for everything . . . but she was asleep before there was time to start working it out.

The next morning it was April and it was spring. Just like that, spring had arrived. The wind dropped, the sun rose into a cloudless sky, the barometer soared and the temperature with it. The air was balmy, soft, smelling of newly-turned earth. The snow melted to nothing, revealing drifts of snowdrops and tiny, early crocuses, and under the beech trees carpets of shiny yellow aconites. Birds sang, doors stood open to the welcome warmth, washing lines billowed with curtains and blankets and other evidence of spring cleaning.

At Rossie Hill, at about ten o'clock in the morning, the telephone began to ring. Duncan Fraser was out, but Liz was in the flower pantry, arranging a vase of pussy-willow sprigs and tall King Alfred daffodils. She put down her secateurs, dried her hands and went to answer the call.

"Hallo?"

"Elizabeth!"

It was her mother from London, sounding expectant, and Liz frowned. She was still smarting from Oliver's abrupt rejection of the night before, and consequently not in the best of moods.

Elaine Haldane, however, was not to know this. "Darling, so extravagant ringing in the morning, but I simply had to know how everything went. I knew you'd never call me. How did the dinner-party go?"

Liz, resigned, pulled up a chair and slumped into it.

"It didn't," she said.

"What do you mean?"

"At the last moment Oliver couldn't come. The dinner-party never happened."

"Oh, dear, how disappointing, and I was longing to hear all about it. You sounded so excited." She waited, and then when her daughter was forthcoming with no more information, added tentatively, "You haven't had a row or anything?"

Liz laughed shortly. "No, of course not. He just couldn't make it. He's busy, I guess. Dad gave him lunch yesterday and they talked business the entire time. Incidentally, Dad's going to buy Cairney."

"Well, that'll keep *him* busy at any rate," Elaine said, in a waspish fashion. "Oh, poor Oliver, what a prospect for him. He's going through a very thin time. You must just be very patient, darling, and *very* understanding."

Liz did not want to talk about Oliver any more. To change the subject she said, "What's happening in the great city?"

"All sorts of things. We're not going back to Paris for another week or two. Parker's involved with some visiting firemen from New York, so we're staying here. It's fun seeing people, hearing all the news. Oh, I know what I *must* tell you. The *most* extraordinary thing has happened."

Liz recognized the gossipy tone in her mother's voice, knew that the telephone call would last for at least another ten minutes. She reached for a cigarette and settled down to listen.

"You know Diana Carpenter, and Shaun? Well, Diana's stepchildren have disappeared. Yes, literally, disappeared. Off the face of the earth. All they left was a letter saying they'd gone to Scotland—of all places—to find their brother Angus. And of course he's the most terrible hippie-type, Diana's had a terribly worrying time with him. Spends his time seeking the truth in India or wherever it is these people think they're going to find it. I would have thought Scotland would be the last place he'd come to, nothing but down-to-earth tweeds and haggis. I must say I always thought Caroline was rather an *odd* girl. She tried to go on the stage once, and it was the most terrible failure, but I never thought she'd do anything so bizarre as simply *disappear.*"

"What's Diana doing about it?"

"My dear, what can she do? And the last thing she wants is to call the police in. After all, although the boy is only a child, the girl *is* supposed to be adult . . . she should be able to look after him. And Diana's terrified of the papers getting on to the story and splashing it all over the front pages of the evening editions. And if that wasn't enough, the wedding's on Tuesday, and Hugh does have a certain professional reputation to maintain."

"Wedding?"

"Caroline's wedding." Elaine sounded exasperated as though Liz was being very stupid. "Caroline is marrying Diana's brother, Hugh Rashley. On Tuesday. The wedding rehearsal's on Monday and they don't even know where she is. It's all too distressing. I always thought she was an odd girl, didn't you?"

"I don't know. I never met her."

"No, of course you haven't. I always forget. Silly of me. But you know I always thought she was rather fond of Diana, I never thought she'd do this to her. Oh, darling, you won't do it to me, will you, when you eventually do get married? And let's hope it's very soon now and to the Right Man. No mentioning names, but you know who I mean. And now I simply must go. I've got a hair appointment and I'm going to be late as it is. And, darling, don't fret about Oliver, just go and see him and be cosy and understanding. I'm sure everything will be all right. And I'm longing to see you. Come back soon."

"I will."

"Goodbye, darling." And then an unconvincing afterthought: "My love to your father."

Later still in the morning Caroline Cliburn lay, supine on a bed of heather, the sun's warmth like a cloak on the length of her body, her arm flung across her eyes against its dazzling brightness. Thus blinded, her other senses became twice as sharp. She heard curlews, the distant cawing of a crow, the lap of water, the tiny sough of some mysterious, unfelt breeze. She smelt the pure sweetness of snow and clear water and earth, mossy and damp and dark with peat. She felt the cool nose of Lisa, the old labrador, who lay beside her, and pressed her nose into Caroline's hand.

Beside her, Oliver Cairney sat, smoking a cigarette, his hands loose between his knees, watching Jody's exertions as the boy struggled, out in the middle of the little loch, with a bulky rowboat and a pair of oars too long for him. Every now and then came an ominous splash, and Caroline would raise her head to investigate, see that he had merely caught a crab, or was driving the rowboat around in small circles, and satisfied that he was not on the point of drowning himself, lie back in the heather and cover her eyes once more.

Oliver said, "If I hadn't tied him up in that life-jacket, you'd be running up and down the bank like a demented hen."

"No, I wouldn't. I'd be out there with him."

"Which would make two of you ripe for drowning." The heather pricked through her shirt, a nameless bug walked up her arm. She sat up, brushing the bug away, screwing her face up into the sunshine.

"You could hardly believe it, could you? Two days ago and Jody and I were in the middle of a blizzard. And now this." The surface of the loch was still and clear, blue as summer with reflected sky. Beyond the distant reed-fringed bank, the moor rose in a series of swelling, heathery slopes, crested at the peak by an outcrop of rock, like a beacon on the top of a mountain. She could see the distant shapes of a flock of grazing sheep, hear in the still morning, their plaintive baaing. The rowboat, so manfully oared, creaked slowly across the surface of the water. Jody's hair stood up on end, and his face was beginning to turn pink.

She said, "It *is* a lovely place. I hadn't realized how lovely it was."

"This is the best time. Now and for another month or two when the beech leaves open and the daffodils come out and all of a sudden it's summer. And then in October, it's beautiful again, the trees flaming out, the sky deep blue and all the heather turned purple."

"Won't you miss it terribly?"

"Of course I will, but there's nothing to be done about it."

"You're going to sell it?"

"Yes." He dropped the stub of his cigarette, stamped it out with the heel of his shoe.

"Have you got a buyer?"

"Yes. Duncan Fraser. My neighbour. He lives across the glen, you can't see his house, because it's hidden by that stand of pines, but he wants the land to take in with his own. It's simply a question of doing away with the march fences."

"And your house?"

"That'll have to go separately. I've got to talk to the lawyers about that. I said I'd go down to Relkirk this afternoon and see them, see if we can thrash something out."

"Won't you keep *any* of Cairney?"

"How you do harp on a subject."

"Men are usually sentimental about tradition, and land."

"Perhaps I am."

"But you don't mind living in London?"

"Good God, no. I love it."

"What do you do?"

"I work for Bankfoot and Balcarries. And if you don't know what they do, they're one of the largest engineering consultants in the country."

"And where do you live?"

"In a flat, just off the Fulham Road."

"Not very far from us." She smiled to think how close they had lived, without ever meeting each other. "It's funny, isn't it? London's so big, and yet you can come to Scotland and meet your next-door neighbour. Is it a nice flat?"

"I like it."

She tried to picture it, but failed utterly because it was impossible to imagine Oliver away from Cairney.

"Is it big or small?"

"Quite big. Big rooms. It's the ground floor of an old house."

"Have you got a garden?"

"Yes. Rather overrun by my neighbour's cat. And a big sitting-room and a kitchen where I eat, and a couple of bedrooms and a bathroom. All mod. cons. in fact, except that my car has to moulder at the pavement's edge in all weathers. Now what else do you want to know?"

"Nothing."

"The colour of the curtains? Crushed elephant's breath." He cupped his hands to his mouth and shouted out across the water. "Hey, Jody!"

Jody paused and looked around, the oars held high and dripping. "I think you've had enough. Come along in now."

"All right."

"That's it. Pull with the left oar. No, the *left*, you idiot! That's the way." He got to his feet and walked down to the end of the wooden jetty and stood waiting for the rowboat's slow, splashy progress to bring it within reach. Then he crouched down to reach for the painter and draw it alongside. Beaming, Jody unshipped the heavy oars, and

Oliver took them and tied up the boat while Jody clambered out. He came back up the jetty towards his sister, and she saw that his sneakers were soaking and his jeans wet to the knee. He was delighted with himself.

"You did very well," Caroline told him.

"I'd have done better if the oars hadn't been so big." He struggled with the knots on the life-jacket and pulled it off over his head. "I've been thinking, Caroline, wouldn't it be nice if we could stay here for ever? It's got everything anybody could want."

Caroline had been thinking this at intervals throughout the morning; and then telling herself, at equal intervals, not to be such a fool. Now, she told Jody not to be a fool, and his face was surprised at the impatience in her voice.

Oliver tightened the rope on the wooden bollard, shouldered the heavy oars and carried them over to the ramshackle boat house to put them away. Jody picked up the life-jacket and went to put that away as well, and they shut the sagging door and came back to Caroline over the springy turf, the tall young man and the freckled boy, with the sun behind them and the dazzle of water.

They reached her side. "Up you get," said Oliver and reached out a hand to pull her to her feet. Lisa scrambled up as well, and stood waving her tail, as if anticipating some pleasant excursion.

"This was meant to be a walk of an exploration or something," Oliver went on. "And all we've done is sit in the sun and watch Jody take all the exercise."

Jody asked, "Where shall we go now?"

"There's something I want to show you . . . it's just round the corner."

They followed him, Indian file, trailing the small sheep tracks that netted the margins of the loch. They crested a rise and the loch took a sharp turn and at its end stood a small, derelict cottage.

"Is that what you wanted to show us?" asked Jody.

"Yes."

"It's a ruin."

"I know. It hasn't been lived in for years. Charles and I used to play here. Once we were even allowed to sleep out."

"Who used to live here?"

"I don't know. A shepherd. Or a crofter. Those little walls are old sheep pens and there's a rowan in the garden. In the old days, country people used to plant rowans at their doors because they thought they brought good fortune."

"I don't know what a rowan looks like."

"In England they call them Mountain Ash. They have feathery leaves and bright red berries, rather like holly."

As they came closer to the house Caroline saw that it was not as derelict as it had first appeared. Stone built, it had retained a certain air of solidity, and although the corrugated iron roof had fallen into disrepair, and the door hung from its hinges, it was clear that it had once been an entirely respectable dwelling, snug in the fold of the hill, with the traces of a garden still visible between the drystone walls. They went up the ghost of the path, and in through the door, Oliver prudently ducking his head beneath the low lintel, and there was one big room, with a rusty iron stove at one end, and a broken chair, and on the floor, the remains of a swallow's nest. The floor was cracked and gaping and stained with bird droppings, and the slanting sun rays danced with motes of dust.

In the corner a rotted ladder led to an upper floor.

"Desirable, detached, two-storey dwelling house," said Oliver. "Who wants to go up?"

Jody wrinkled his nose. "I don't." He was secretly afraid of spiders. "I'm going back to the garden. I want to look at the rowan tree. Come along, Lisa, you come with me."

So Oliver and Caroline were left alone to mount the rotting ladder, which was missing more rungs than it had kept. They climbed into a loft that was splashed with sunlight that poured through the holes in the gaping roof. The floor planks were rotten and breaking, but the crossbeams beneath them sound, and there was just space for Oliver to stand erect, in the very centre of the room, with the top of his head only half an inch from the ridgepole.

Caroline stuck her head cautiously out of one of the holes in the roof and saw Jody in the garden below, swinging like a monkey from a branch of the rowan. She saw the curving length of the loch, the green of the first of the farm fields, cattle grazing, brown and white like toys, and in the far distance, the line of the main road. She withdrew her head and turned to Oliver. He had a cobweb on his chin and he said in Cockney, "Ow about it, lidy? With a lick of paint you won't know the place?"

"But you couldn't do anything with it, could you? Seriously."

"I don't know. It just occurred to me that perhaps it would be possible. If I can sell Cairney House then I could maybe afford to spend some money on this place."

"But there's no running water."

"I could fix that."

"Or drains."

"Septic tank."

"Or electricity."

"Lamps. Candles. Much more flattering."

"And what would you cook on?"

"Calor gas."

"And when would you use it?"

"Week-ends. Holidays. I could bring my children here."

"I didn't know you had any."

"I haven't yet. That I know of. But when I get married, it would be a desirable little property to have under my belt. It would also mean that I still owned a little bit of Cairney. Which should set your sentimental heart at rest."

"So it does matter to you."

"Caroline, life is too short to look back over your shoulder. You only lose the way and stumble and probably fall flat on your face. I'd rather look forward."

"But this house . . ."

"It was just an idea. I thought it might amuse you to see it. Come on now, we must get back or Mrs Cooper will think we're all drowned."

He went first down the ladder, cautiously feeling for each surviving rung before he put his weight on it. At the bottom he waited for Caroline, holding the ladder steady between his hands. But half-way down, she became stranded, unable either to go up or down. She started to laugh and he told her to jump, and she said that she couldn't jump, and Oliver said any fool could jump, but by then Caroline was laughing too much to do anything constructive, and finally, inevitably, she slipped, there was the ominous crack of rotted wood, and her descent finished in an undignified slither before Oliver finally caught her in his arms.

There was a sprig of heather in her pale hair, her sweater felt warm from the sunshine, and the long sleep of the night before had wiped the smudges from beneath her eyes. Her skin was smooth and faintly pink, her face turned up to his, her mouth open in laughter. Without thought, without hesitation, he bent and kissed her. Suddenly, it was very quiet. For an instant she stayed still, and then she put the palms of her hands against his chest and pushed him gently away. The laughter had gone from her face, and there was an expression in her eyes that he had never seen there before.

She said at last, "It was just the day."

"What's that meant to mean?"

"Part of a nice day. The sunshine. Spring."

"Does that make any difference?"

"I don't know."

She moved away from him, out of his arms, turned and went towards the door. She stood there, leaning a shoulder against the doorpost, silhouetted against the light, her tangled hair an aureole about the neat shape of her head.

She said, "It's a darling house. I think you should keep it."

Jody had abandoned the rowan, had been lured back to the water's edge, was skimming stones trying to make them jump, and driving Lisa insane because she didn't know whether she was meant to plunge in and retrieve them, or stay where she was. Caroline picked up a flat pebble and threw it and it jumped three times before it sank out of sight.

Jody was furious. "I wish you'd show me. Show me how you do it," but Caroline turned away from him because she couldn't reply, and she didn't want him to see her face. Because all at once she knew why she had fallen out of love with the memory of Drennan Colefield. And, which was much more frightening, she knew why she had not told Oliver that she was going to marry Hugh.

Liz, coming to Cairney, found it quiet and apparently deserted. She stopped her car at the door, killed the engine and waited for someone to come out and greet her. Nobody did. But the door stood open, so she got out of the car and went indoors and stood in the middle of the hall and said Oliver's name. Still no response, but domestic noises came from the direction of the kitchen, and familiar as she was with the house, Liz took herself down the passage and through the swing door, and surprised Mrs Cooper who had just come indoors from hanging out a line of clothes.

She started elaborately, and placed her hand over her heart. "Liz!" She had known Liz since she was a child and would never have thought of calling her Miss Fraser.

"Sorry. I didn't mean to frighten you. I thought the house was deserted."

"Oliver's out. He took . . . the others with him." There was only the slightest hesitation but Liz latched on to it at once. She raised her eyebrows.

"You mean your unexpected visitors? I've been hearing all about them."

"Och, they're just a couple of youngsters. Oliver took them down to the loch, the wee boy wanted to see the boat." She looked up at the kitchen clock. "But they'll be back any time, they're having an early dinner, for Oliver has to get back to Relkirk this afternoon to have another wee chat with the lawyer. Will you wait? Will you stay for lunch?"

"I won't stay for lunch, but I'll wait a moment, and if they don't come, I'll go home. I only came to see how Oliver was getting on."

"He's really been great," Mrs Cooper told her. "In a way all this happening has been a good thing, taken his mind off his loss."

"All this?" Liz prompted gently.

"Well, the young ones turning up like that, with their car broken down and nowhere to go."

"They came by car?"

"Yes, drove from London seemingly. The car was in a terrible mess, right in the ditch, and on top of that frozen solid after a night in the open. But Cooper took it down to the garage, and they phoned early this morning and he went to pick it up and bring it back. It's in the shed at the back of the house now, all ready for when they want to go away again."

"When are they going?" Liz kept her voice casual and very cool.

"I couldn't be sure. Nothing's been said to me. There's some talk about their brother staying in Strathcorrie, but he's away just now, and I think they're hoping to wait until he gets back." She added, "But if you see Oliver, he'll give you all the news himself. They're just down at the loch. If you wanted, you could start off and meet them half way."

"Maybe I'll do that," said Liz.

But she didn't. She went back outside and settled herself on the stone bench outside the library window, put on her dark glasses, lit a cigarette and stretched out her body to the sun.

It was very quiet, so that she heard their voices in the still morning air long before they actually appeared. The garden path curved away around the perimeter of a beech hedge, and as they came around this, into view, they seemed engrossed in conversation and did not immediately see Liz sitting there, waiting for them. The small boy led the way, and a pace or two behind him, Oliver, in an ancient tweed jacket and with red cotton handkerchief knotted at his throat, pulled the girl along by the hand, as though she had become tired from the walk and started to lag behind.

He was talking. Liz heard the deep tones of his voice without being able to catch the words. Then the girl halted, and bent over, as if to ease a stone out of her shoe. A long curtain of pale hair fell across her face, and Oliver stopped, too, to wait for her, patient, his dark head bent down, her hand still in his. And Liz saw this and all at once she was afraid. She felt she was being shut out of something, as though the three of them were in some sort of a conspiracy against her. The stone was finally removed. Oliver turned to resume the climb, and then caught sight of the dark blue Triumph parked in front of the house. He saw Liz. She dropped her cigarette and stubbed it out under the heel of her shoe and stood up and went to meet them, but Oliver had let go of the girl's hand and strode out ahead of the others, taking the steep grassy bank at a run, and meeting Liz at the top.

"Liz."

"Hallo, Oliver."

He thought that she looked better than ever, in tight buff pants and a fringed leather jacket. He took her hands and kissed her. He said, "Have you come to give me hell about last night?"

"No," said Liz frankly, and her eyes looked over his shoulder to where Caroline and Jody, more slowly, were coming over the grass. "I told you I was intrigued by your sudden rash of house guests. I've come to say how do you do."

"We went down to the loch." He turned towards the others. "Caroline, this is Liz Fraser, she and her father are my nearest neighbours and she's been in and out of Cairney since she was knee-high to a grasshopper. I showed you their house this morning, through the trees. Liz, this is Caroline Cliburn, and this is Jody."

"How do you do," said Caroline. They shook hands. Liz took off her dark glasses, and it was with something of a shock that Caroline saw the expression in the other girl's eyes.

"Hallo," said Liz. And then, "Hallo, Jody."

"How do you do," said Jody.

Oliver asked, "Have you been here long?"

She turned to him, away from the other two. "Ten minutes, perhaps. No longer."

"You'll stay for lunch?"

"Mrs Cooper very sweetly asked me, but I'm expected home."

"Then come in and have a drink."

"No, I must get back. I only dropped by to say hallo." She smiled at Caroline. "Mrs Cooper's been telling me all about you. She says you've got a brother staying at Strathcorrie."

"He's not been there long . . ."

"Perhaps I've met him. What's his name?"

Without knowing why, Caroline hesitated, and Jody, catching the hesitation, answered the question for her.

"He's called Cliburn, like us," he told Liz. "Angus Cliburn."

After lunch Oliver, swearing at the necessity, on such a beautiful afternoon, of having to change into a respectable suit and a collar and tie, get into his car, drive to the town and spend the rest of the day incarcerated in a stuffy lawyer's office, duly departed.

Caroline and Jody saw him away, waving him down the drive. When the car had gone out of sight, they still stood there, listening to the sound of his engine as it paused at the main road, and then swung out, changed up, and roared up and away over the hill.

He was gone, and they found themselves slightly at a loss. Mrs Cooper, her dishes washed and wiped, had gone home to look after her own house and get a load of washing out on to the line before the warmth went out of the day. Jody kicked disconsolately at the gravel. Caroline watched him in sympathy, knowing just how he felt.

"What do you want to do?"

"I don't know."

"Do you want to go back to the loch?"

"I don't know." He was any small boy, suddenly bereft of his best friend.

"We could do another jigsaw."

"Not indoors."

109

"We could bring it out and do it in the sun."

"I don't feel like doing jigsaws."

Defeated, Caroline went to sit on the bench where they had found Liz Fraser waiting for them this morning. She found that her thoughts instinctively shied from the memory of the encounter, and so, deliberately, she made herself go back, go over it, try to decide why she had found the other girl's sudden appearance so disturbing.

It was, after all, entirely natural. She was obviously a very old friend, a close neighbour, she appeared to have known Oliver all his life. Her father was buying Cairney. What could be more normal than she should drive over to make a friendly call and meet Oliver's guests?

But still, there was something there. A violent antipathy which Caroline had felt the moment Liz took off her dark glasses and looked her straight in the eye. Jealousy, perhaps? But, surely she had nothing to be jealous of. She was a hundred times more attractive than Caroline and Oliver was obviously devoted to her. Or perhaps she was simply possessive, as a sister might be? But this still did not account for the fact that standing, talking to her, Caroline had been left with the impression that, layer by layer, she was being slowly stripped of every garment she wore.

Jody was squatting, scooping gravel into small mounds with hands that were grey with dust. He looked up.

"Someone's coming," he said.

They listened. He was right. A car had turned in at the foot of the avenue, was now approaching the house.

"Perhaps Oliver's forgotten something."

But it wasn't Oliver. It was the same dark blue Triumph that had stood outside the house this morning; its hood down, and Liz Fraser, with her glinting hair and her dark glasses, and a silk scarf around her neck, was at the wheel. Instinctively, both Caroline and Jody stood up, and the car rammed to a stop not two yards from where they waited, a cloud of dust flying from the back wheels.

"Hallo again," said Liz and switched off the engine.

Jody said nothing. His face was blank. Caroline said "Hallo" and Liz opened the door and got out and slammed the door shut behind her. She took off her glasses and Caroline saw that her eyes were not smiling although her mouth was. "Oliver gone?"

"Yes, about ten minutes ago."

Liz smiled at Jody and reached over into the back of her car. "I brought you a present. I thought you might be running out of things to do." She produced a small-size putter and a golf ball. "There used to be a putting-green on that flat bit of lawn. I'm sure if you look you'll find the hole and some of the markers. Do you like putting?"

Jody's face lit up. He adored presents. "Oh, thank you. I don't know. I've never done it."

"It's fun. Very tricky. Why don't you go and see how good you are?"

"Thank you," he said again, and started off. Half-way down the bank he turned. "When I've learned how, will you come and have a game with me?"

"Of course I will. We'll have a little bet and see who wins the prize."

He went, running down the last of the slope on to the level lawn. Liz turned to Caroline and let her smile die. She said, "I really came to have a little talk with you. Shall we sit down? It's so much more restful."

They sat, Caroline wary, Liz very much at ease, reaching for a cigarette, lighting it with a tiny gold lighter. She said, "I had a telephone call from my mother."

Caroline had nothing to say to this bit of gratuitous information. Liz went on, "You don't know who I am, do you? I mean, apart from being Liz Fraser who lives at Rossie Hill?" Caroline shook her head. "But you know Elaine and Parker Haldane." Caroline nodded. "My dear, don't look so blank. Elaine's my mother."

Looking back, Caroline could not imagine how she had been so dense. Elizabeth. Liz. Scotland. She remembered at that last dinner-party in London, Elaine talking about Elizabeth. *Well, you know, ten years ago when Duncan and I were still together, we bought this place in Scotland.* Duncan, Liz's father, who was going to buy Cairney from Oliver. *And the first thing Elizabeth did was to make friends with the two boys who lived on the neighbouring estate . . . the older brother . . . killed himself in a terrible car smash.*

And she remembered Jody telling her about Charles being killed, and how a memory had stirred in her subconscious, and yet been forgotten before it had come to conscious light.

The pieces had been scattered, like the pieces of Jody's undone jigsaw, but they had been there, right in front of her nose, only she had been too stupid, or perhaps too involved in her own problems, to fit them all together.

She said, "I've always known you as Elizabeth."

"My mother and Parker call me that, but here I've always been Liz."

"I never realized. I simply never realized."

"Well, there it is. Coincidence and a small world and all that. And, as I say, my mother phoned this morning."

Her eyes were knowing. "What did she tell you?" asked Caroline.

"Well, everything, I suppose. About you and . . . Jody, is it? . . . disappearing. Diana frantic with worry, knowing merely that you are in Scotland, nothing else. And a big wedding next Tuesday. You're marrying Hugh Rashley."

"Yes," said Caroline flatly, for there seemed nothing else to say.

"You appear to have got yourself in something of a mess."

"Yes," said Caroline. "I think I probably have."

"My mother said you'd come to Scotland to find Angus. Wasn't that rather a wild-goose chase?"

"It didn't seem so at the time. It was just that Jody wanted to see Angus again. Because Diana and Shaun want to take Jody to Canada with them and Jody doesn't want to go. And Hugh doesn't want Jody living with us, so that only leaves Angus."

"I thought Angus was a hippie?"

All Caroline's instincts urged her to spring to her brother's defence, but in truth it was hard to think of anything to say. She shrugged. "He is our brother."

"And living at Strathcorrie?"

"Working there. In the hotel."

"But not at the moment?"

"No, but he should be back by tomorrow."

"And you and Jody are going to wait here until he comes?"

"I . . . I don't know."

"You sound uncertain. Perhaps I can help you, make up your mind for you. Oliver's going through a bad time. I don't know whether you realized this. He was devoted to Charles, there were only the two of them. And now Charles is dead and Cairney has to go and this is the end of the line for Oliver. Don't you think, under the circumstances, it would perhaps be . . . considerate if you and your brother were to go back to London? For Oliver's sake. And Diana's. And Hugh's."

Caroline was not deceived. "Why do you want us out of the way?"

Liz was unperturbed. "Perhaps because you're an embarrassment to Oliver."

"Because of you?"

Liz smiled. "Oh, my dear, we've known each other so long, we're very close. Closer than you could imagine. That's one of the reasons my father's buying Cairney."

"You're going to marry him?"

"Of course."

"He never said."

"Why should he? Did you tell him that you were going to be married? Or perhaps it's a secret? I notice you don't wear an engagement ring."

"I . . . I left it in London. It's too big for me and I'm always afraid of losing it."

"But he doesn't know, does he?"

"No."

"That's funny, not telling Oliver. After all, according to my mother, it's going to be a very large affair. I suppose a well-to-do stockbroker like Hugh Rashley would consider it part and parcel of his successful image. You are still going to marry him? But for some reason you don't want Oliver to know?" And then when Caroline did not reply to any of these queries, she began to laugh. "My dear child, I do believe you've fallen in love with him. Well, I don't blame you at all. I'm very sorry for you. But I'm on your side, so I'll make a little bargain. You and Jody go back to London, and I shan't breathe a word to Oliver about your wedding. He won't know a thing about it until he sees the newspapers on Wednesday morning, which will doubtless carry the whole story, with a picture of the pair of you at the church door, looking like something that came off the top of a wedding cake. How's that? No explanations, no excuses. Just a clean break. Back to your Hugh who obviously adores you, and leave hippie Angus to his own devices. Now, doesn't that make sense?"

Caroline said, helplessly, "There's Jody . . ."

"He's a child. A little boy. He'll adapt. He'll go to Canada and love it, be captain of the ice hockey team in no time. Diana's the best person to take care of him, you can surely see that? Someone like Angus could be nothing but the worst possible influence. Oh, Caroline, come off your cloud and face facts. Throw the whole thing over and go back to London."

From the lawn below them came a triumphant yell as Jody finally got the golf ball into the hole. He appeared up the bank, running, brandishing his new club. "I've got the hang of it. You have to hit it quite slowly and not too hard, and . . ." He stopped. Liz was on her feet, was pulling on her gloves. "Aren't you going to play with me?"

"Another time," said Liz.

"But you said."

"Another time." She got into her car, neatly stowing her long legs. "Right now your sister has something she wants to tell you."

Oliver drove home through the blue dusk of the perfect day, his mood quite different from that of the day before. Now, he was relaxed, and for some reason, oddly content. Not exhausted by the long legal interview; clear-headed and much happier now that he had actually taken the final step of putting Cairney House up for sale. He had spoken, too, to the lawyer, about keeping the Loch Cottage, renovating it and converting it to a small holiday house, and the lawyer had raised no objections, provided Oliver could make arrangements with Duncan Fraser for an access road through what would become, in the course of time, Duncan's land.

Oliver did not imagine that Duncan would raise any objections to this. The thought of the house, raised square and sturdy again, filled him with satisfaction. He would take the garden down to the water's edge, open up the old hearth, re-build the chimney, put dormer windows in the loft. Planning, he began to whistle to himself. The leather wheel felt firm and pleasant beneath his hands and the car took the curves of the familiar road easily, sweetly, like a steeplechaser. As though, like Oliver, it knew it was coming home.

He turned in at the gates and roared up the drive beneath the trees, coming around the sweep by the rhododendrons with a flourish on his horn to let Jody and Caroline know that he was safely back. He left the car by the front door and went indoors taking off his coat, and waiting for Jody's footsteps.

But the house was silent. He put his coat down across a chair and called, "Jody!" There was no reply. "Caroline!" Still nothing. He went down to the kitchen but it was dark and empty. Mrs Cooper had not yet come in to start cooking supper. Puzzled, he let the door swing shut and went along to the library. This, too, he found dark, the fire dying in the hearth. He switched on the light and went over to throw on some fresh logs. He straightened and saw the envelope on his desk, a square of white propped against the telephone. One of the best envelopes out of the top drawer in his desk, and on it was written his name.

He opened it and saw, to his surprise, that his hands were shaking. He unfolded the single sheet and read Caroline's letter.

Dear Oliver,

After you had gone Jody and I talked things over and we have decided that it would be best if we go back to London. It isn't any good waiting for Angus, we don't know when he will be back and it isn't fair on Diana to stay longer when she doesn't even know where we are.

Please don't worry about us. The car is working beautifully and your kind garage filled it up with petrol for us. I don't think there will be any more blizzards and I'm sure we shall get back safely.

There isn't any way of saying thank you, to you and Mrs Cooper, for all you have done. We loved being at Cairney. We shall never forget it.

With love from us both,
Caroline.

7

The next morning, pretending to himself that he wanted to square off one or two problems with Duncan Fraser, Oliver drove himself over to Rossie Hill. It was another beautiful day, but colder; over the night there had been the lightest of frosts, and the sun had not yet enough warmth to melt this away, but still the Rossie Hill drive was lined with the bobbing heads of the first early daffodils and when he went into the house it smelt of the great bowl of blue hyacinths which stood in the middle of the table in the hall.

As familiar with this house as Liz was with Cairney, he searched for occupants, running Liz to earth at last in her father's study, where she sat on the desk and conducted a telephone conversation. To the butcher by the sound of it. When he opened the door she looked up, saw him, raised her eyebrows in a silent message to tell him to wait. He came into the room and went to stand by the fire, wanting a cigarette and yet not wanting one, comforted by the warmth of the flames against the front of his legs.

She finished the phone call and hung up, but stayed by the telephone, very still, one long leg swinging thoughtfully. She wore a pleated skirt, a skinny sweater, a silk scarf knotted round the base of her throat. The skin of her arms and her face still glowed from the Antigua sun, and for a long moment her dark eyes met his across the room.

116

Then she said, "Looking for somebody?"

"Your father."

"He's out. Gone to Relkirk. Won't be back till lunchtime." She reached for a silver cigarette-box and held it out to him. Oliver shook his head, so she took one for herself and lit it from the heavy desk lighter. She surveyed him thoughtfully through a drift of blue smoke. She said, "You look a little distrait, Oliver. Is anything wrong?"

He had been trying all morning to tell himself that nothing was wrong, but now he said bluntly, "Caroline and Jody have gone."

"Gone?" Her voice was mildly surprised. "Where have they gone?"

"Back to London. I got back last night and found a letter from Caroline."

"But surely that's quite a good thing."

"After all that, they never got to find their brother."

"From what I could gather, that doesn't sound as though it'll make much difference either way."

"But it mattered to them. It mattered to Jody."

"Provided you think they're capable of getting themselves back to London I shouldn't worry too much about them. You've got enough on your plate without acting as Nanny to a couple of lame dogs you'd never even seen before." She changed the subject, as though it were of little importance. "What did you want to see my father about?"

He could scarcely remember. ". . . an access road. I want to keep the Loch Cottage if I can, but I'll need access up the glen."

"Keep the Loch Cottage? But it's a ruin."

"Basically, it's sound enough. Just needs a bit of tidying up, a new roof."

"And what do you want the Loch Cottage for?"

He said, "To keep. A holiday house, perhaps. I don't know. Just to keep."

"Was it I who put that idea into your head?"

"Perhaps it was."

She slipped off the desk then, and came across the room to stand beside him. "Oliver, I have a better idea."

"And what is that?"

"Let my father buy Cairney House."

Oliver laughed. "He doesn't even want it."

"No, but I do. I would like to have it for . . . what was it you said? Holidays. Week-ends."

"And what would you do with it?"

She tossed her cigarette on the fire. "I would bring my husband here, and my children."

"Would they like that?"

"I don't know. You tell me."

Her eyes were clear, honest, unblinking. He was astonished by what she was saying and yet flattered too. And amazed. Little Liz, leggy, gawky Liz, all grown up and composed as hell and asking Oliver to . . .

He said, "Forgive me if I'm all wrong, but oughtn't I to be the one who comes up with these sorts of ideas?"

"Yes, I suppose you should. But I've known you too long to indulge in coy dishonesties. And I have this feeling that our coming together again like this, when neither of us expected to find each other, is meant. Part of a pattern. I have this feeling that Charles meant it to happen."

"But it was always Charles who loved you."

"That's what I mean. And Charles is dead."

"Would you have married him, if he'd lived?"

Her answer was to put her arms round his neck and pull down his head and kiss him on the mouth. For a second he hesitated, taken off his guard, but only for a second. She was Liz, scented, dazzling, marvellously attractive. He put his arms round her and drew her close, her slender body pressed against his, and told himself that perhaps she was right. Perhaps this was the direction his life was meant to go, and perhaps this was what Charles had always meant to happen.

He was, not unnaturally, late home for lunch. The kitchen was reproachfully empty, his single place laid at the table, a good smell of cooking coming from the stove. Searching for Mrs Cooper he found her in the nursery, stacking away all the old toys that Jody had left disarranged, and looking like a mother who has been bereft of her children.

He put his head around the door and said, "I'm late, I'm sorry."

She looked up from the box of bricks which she was meticulously packing. "Och, it doesn't matter." She sounded listless. "It's only a shepherd's pie. I left it in the cool oven, you can eat it when you feel like it."

She had been shocked and much distressed last night when he told her that the Cliburns had gone. From her expression now he knew that she had not yet got over this. He said, robustly, trying to cheer her, "They should be well on their way by now. In London by this evening, if there's not too much traffic on the roads."

Mrs Cooper sniffed. "I just can't bear the feel of the house without them. It's as though that wee boy had lived here the whole of his life. It was like Cairney coming alive again, having him here."

"I know." Oliver was sympathetic. "But they'd have had to go in a day or two anyway."

"And it wasn't even as though I had the chance to say goodbye to them." She made it sound as though it were all Oliver's fault.

"I know." He could think of nothing else to say.

"And he never got to see his brother. He talked so much about his brother Angus, and then he never even got to see him. It just makes me heart sick."

This, from Mrs Cooper, was strong language. All at once Oliver felt as depressed as she was. He said, feebly, "I . . . I'll go and eat that shepherd's pie," and then, at the door, remembered why he had originally come in search of her. "Oh, Mrs Cooper, don't bother to come in this evening. I've been asked to dinner at Rossie Hill . . ."

She acknowledged this with a nod, as though too distressed to say another word. Oliver left her to her disconsolate tidying and went downstairs again, and felt the house watchful and silent, as though, bereft of Jody's noisy presence, it had sunk into a gloom as thick as Mrs Cooper's own.

Rossie Hill, made ready for a dinner-party, was as bright and glowing as the inside of a jewel-box. When Oliver let himself into the house, he smelt the hyacinths, saw the flickering of logs in the grate, was immediately soothed by warmth and comfort. As he took off his coat and dropped it over the chair in the hall, Liz emerged from the kitchen, carrying a bowl of ice-cubes in her hand. She stopped when she saw him, her smile sudden and brilliant.

"Oliver."

"Hallo."

He took her shoulders between his hands and kissed her carefully, cautious about blurring the clear line of her lipstick. She both smelt and tasted delicious. He held her off, the better to admire her. She wore red, a silk trouser dress with a high collar, and diamonds sparked from her neatly-set ears. She reminded him of a parakeet, a bird of paradise, all bright eyes and glittering plumage.

He said, "I'm early."

"Not early. Just right. The others haven't come yet."

He raised his eyebrows. "Others?"

"I told you it was a dinner-party." He followed her through to the drawing-room where she set down the ice-bowl on a meticulously pre-pared drink table. "The Allfords. Do you know them? They've come to live in Relkirk. He's something to do with whisky. They're longing to meet you. Now, shall I pour you a drink or would you rather do it yourself? I do mix a very special Martini."

"Where did you learn to do that?"

"Oh, I picked it up on my travels."

"Would I be ungracious if I opted for a whisky and soda?"

"Not ungracious at all, just typically Scottish."

She poured it for him, just the way he liked it, not too dark, bubbling, bobbing with ice. She brought it over and he took it, and he kissed her again. She detached herself reluctantly, and went back to the drink table and began to mix a jug of Martinis.

While she did, they were joined by Duncan, and then the front-door bell rang, and Liz went out to greet her other guests.

When she was out of the room Duncan said to Oliver, "Liz has told me."

Oliver was surprised. Nothing definite had been settled this morning. Nothing discussed. His talk with Liz, though filled with de-light, had been more of the past, remembering, than of the future. It had seemed to Oliver that there was all the time in the world to decide about the future.

He said, carefully, "What did she say?"

"Nothing very much. Just put one or two ideas in my way, as it were. But you have to know, Oliver, that nothing would make me a happier man."

"I . . . I'm glad."

"And as for Cairney . . ." Voices approached the half open door, and he broke off abruptly. "We'll talk about it later."

* * *

120

The Allfords were middle-aged, the husband large and ponderous, the wife very slender, pink-and-white with the soft, fluffy blonde hair that looks so colourless when it starts to go grey. Everybody was introduced, and Oliver found himself sitting by Mrs Allford on the sofa, hearing about her children who hadn't wanted to come and live in Scotland but now loved it. About her daughter who lived for the local Pony Club, and her son who was in his first year at Cambridge.

"And you . . . now you live next door, if that's the right term to use."

"No. I live in London."

"But . . ."

"My brother, Charles Cairney, lived at Cairney but he was killed in a car smash. I'm just up here trying to get all his affairs sorted out."

"Oh, of course." Mrs Allford put on a face suitable for tragedy. "I did know. I am sorry. It's so difficult to keep track of everybody when you're meeting them all for the first time."

His attention wandered back to Liz. Her father and Mr Allford were standing, deep in business talk. She stood beside them, holding her drink and a small dish of salted nuts from which Mr Allford, absently, helped himself from time to time. She felt Oliver's gaze and turned towards him. He winked with the eye farthest from Mrs Allford and Liz smiled.

Finally, they went in to dinner, the dining-room softly lit, velvet curtains drawn against the night. There were lace mats on dark shining wood, crystal and silver, a mass of scarlet tulips, the same red as Liz's dress, in the middle of the table. Then smoked salmon, pink and delectable, white wine, escalopes de veau, tiny brussels sprouts cooked with chestnuts, a pudding that was simply a froth of lemon and cream. Then coffee and brandy, the smell of Havana cigars. Oliver pushed back his chair, replete and sleek with the comforts of good living, and settled down to the after-dinner conversation.

Behind him the clock on the mantelpiece struck nine o'clock. Some time during the day he had pushed the thought of Jody and Caroline into the back of his mind, and had had no bother with them since. But as the chimes gently rang out he was, all at once, no longer at Rossie Hill, but in London with Cliburns. By now they would be home, tired and weary, trying to explain to Diana, trying to tell her all the things that had happened; Caroline would be exhausted and pale after the long drive, Jody still consumed with disappointment. *We went to find Angus. We went all the way to Scotland to find Angus but he wasn't there. And I don't want to go to Canada.*

And Diana, frantic, scolding, finally forgiving, heating milk for Jody and getting him to bed; and Caroline going upstairs, a step at a time, her face curtained by her long hair, her hand trailing on the banister.

". . . what do you say, Oliver?"

"Uh?" They were all looking at him. "I'm sorry, I wasn't paying attention."

"We were talking about the salmon fishing rights on the Corrie, there's some talk of . . ."

Duncan's voice trailed away. Nobody else spoke. It was suddenly very quiet, and through the stillness they heard what Duncan's sharp ears had heard already. The sound of a car, not on the road, but coming up the hill towards the house. A van, or a lorry; gears crashing down as the incline steepened, and then a flash of headlights against the outside of the drawn curtains, and the steady throb of an ancient engine.

Duncan looked at Liz. "It sounds," he said, making a joke of it, "as though you're expecting the coalman."

She frowned. "I expect it's someone lost the way. Mrs Douglas will go to the door," and smoothly she turned once more to Mr Allford, intending to carry on with the conversation, ignoring the un-known caller who waited outside. But Oliver's attention was drawn as tight as a rubber band, his ears pricked like a dog's. He heard the ringing of the front-door bell, and slow footsteps go to answer the summons. He heard a voice, high and excited, interrupted by Mrs Douglas's mild objects. ". . . canna go in there, there's a dinner-party . . ." And then an exclamation, "Ah, ye wee divil . . ." and the next moment the dining-room door was flung open and outside, poised, his eyes searching the room for the only person he wanted to find, was Jody Cliburn.

Oliver was on his feet, his napkin flung on the table.

"Jody!"

"Oh, *Oliver.*"

He came across the room like a bullet, like a homing pigeon, straight into Oliver's arms.

* * *

The urbane formality of the dinner-party collapsed instantly, like a pricked balloon. The shambles that resulted would have been funny had it not been tragic. For Jody was in tears, bawling like a baby, with his head butted into Oliver's stomach and his arms clutched tight about Oliver's waist as though he had no intention of ever letting him go. Mrs Douglas, harassed in her pinafore, hovered in the doorway, undecided as to whether or not she should come into the dining-room and bodily haul the intruder away. Duncan was on his feet, with no idea of what was happening or who this child could be. From time to time he said, "What the devil is all this about?" but nobody was in a position to give him any sort of a reply. Liz was also on her feet, but saying nothing, simply staring at the back of Jody's head as though, given half a chance, she would like to have smashed it, like some rotten fruit, against the nearest stone wall. Only the Allfords, conventional to the last, stayed where they were, Mr Allford saying, "Extraordinary thing to happen," between puffs of his cigar. "Do you mean to say he's come in the coal lorry?" While Mrs Allford smiled sociably, giving the impression that unknown children had disrupted every memorable dinner-party she had ever been to.

From the depths of Oliver's waistcoat came sobs and snuffles and garbled sentences of which he could neither hear nor understand one word. It was obvious that the situation could not be allowed to continue, but Jody clung so tightly that it was impossible for Oliver to move.

"Now come along," he said at last, raising his voice to make himself heard above the sobs. "Loosen off. We'll go outside and you can tell me what this is about . . ." His words somehow got through to Jody, who loosened his stranglehold slightly and allowed himself to be led towards the door. "So sorry," said Oliver as he went. "Please excuse me for a moment . . . rather unexpected."

Feeling as though he had accomplished a brilliant escape he found himself out in the hall, and Mrs Douglas, bless her good heart, was closing the door behind them.

"Will you be all right?" she whispered.

"We're fine."

She went back to her kitchen, muttering away under her breath, and Oliver sat on a carved wooden chair that had never been built for sitting in and pulled Jody close between his knees. "Stop crying. Try to stop crying. Here, blow your nose and stop crying." Scarlet-faced, swollen, Jody made a valiant effort, but the tears still came.

"I c-can't."

"What's happened?"

"Caroline's ill. She's really ill. She's sick like she was before, and she's got a terrible pain here." Jody laid his own grubby hands over his stomach. "And it's getting worse."

"Where is she?"

"At the Strathcorrie Hotel."

"But she said you were going back to London."

"I wouldn't let her." Tears filled his eyes again. "I w-wanted to find Angus."

"Has Angus come back yet?"

Jody shook his head. "No. There wasn't anybody but you."

"Have you told a doctor?"

"I . . . I didn't know what to do. I c-came to find you . . ."

"You think she's really sick?"

Speechless with crying Jody nodded again. Behind Oliver, the dining-room door quietly opened and shut again. He turned and saw Liz standing there. She said to Jody, "Why didn't you go back to London?" but he saw the anger in her face and he wouldn't answer. "You said you were going back. Your sister said she was taking you back." Her voice was suddenly shrill. "She said . . ."

Oliver stood up, and Liz stopped, as though he had turned off a tap. He turned back to Jody. "Who brought you here?"

"A m-man. A man in a van."

"Go out and wait with him. Tell him I'll be out in a moment . . ."

"But we have to *hurry*."

Oliver raised his voice. "I said I'd be out in a moment." He turned Jody round, gave him a push. "Go on, scoot. Tell him you've found me."

Dejected, Jody went, struggling with the handle of the big door and slamming it shut behind him. Oliver looked at Liz. He said, "The reason they didn't go to London was because Jody wanted a last chance of finding his brother. And now Caroline's ill. That's all there is to it, I'm sorry." He crossed the hall to collect his coat. Behind him Liz said, "Don't go."

He turned, frowning. "But I have to."

124

"Phone the doctor in Strathcorrie, he'll take care of her."

"Liz, I must go."

"Is she that important to you?"

He started to deny this and then found that he didn't want to. "I don't know. Perhaps she is." He began to put on his coat.

"And what about us? You and I?"

He could only repeat himself. "I have to go, Liz."

"If you walk out on me now, you don't ever need to come back."

It sounded like a challenge—or a bluff. Either way it did not seem to be very important. He tried to be gentle. "Don't start saying things you'll only regret."

"Who says I'll regret them?" She wrapped her arms across her chest, holding her upper arms so tightly that the knuckles on her brown hands showed white. She looked as though she were suddenly very cold, as though she were trying to hold herself together. "If you don't watch out, you're going to be the one with the regrets. She's going to be married, Oliver."

He had put on his coat. He said, "Is she, Liz?" and started to do up the buttons and his calm drove her over the edge of her own control.

"She didn't tell you? How extraordinary! Oh, yes, she's getting married on Tuesday. In London. To a very up-and-coming young stockbroker called Hugh Rashley. It's funny you never guessed. But of course she didn't wear an engagement ring, did she? She said it was too big and that she was frightened of losing it, but that seems a little farfetched to me. Aren't you going to ask me how I know all this, Oliver?"

Oliver said, "How do you know it?"

"My mother told me. On the telephone yesterday morning. You see, Diana Carpenter is just about her dearest friend, so of course my mother knows it all."

He said, "Liz, I have to go."

"If you have already lost your heart," she told him sweetly, "take my advice and don't lose your head as well. There's no future in it. You'll only make a fool of yourself."

He said, "Explain to your father for me. Tell him what's happened. Tell him how sorry I am." He opened the door. "Goodbye, Liz."

She could not believe that he wouldn't turn and come back to her, and take her in his arms and tell her that none of this had happened, that he would love her as Charles had loved her, that Caroline Cliburn could take care of herself.

But he didn't. And then he had gone.

The man in the van was a large, red-faced individual in a checked cloth "bunnet." He looked like a farmer and his van smelt of pig manure but he had waited patiently for Oliver to emerge and kept Jody company into the bargain.

Oliver put his head in at the window. "I am sorry to have kept you waiting."

"Nae bother, sir, I'm no' in any hurry at all."

"It was very good of you to bring the boy, I'm most grateful. I hope you didn't have to come far out of your way."

"Not at all. I was on my way down the glen from Strathcorrie in any case. I'd just dropped in for a dram when the wee boy asked me to bring him to Cairney. He seemed a wee bittie upset, and I didna like to leave him there on the roadside." He turned to Jody, patted his knee with a large hamlike hand. "Ach, but you'll be fine now, laddie, now you've found Mr Cairney."

Jody got out of the van. "Thank you *so* much. I don't know what I would have done if you hadn't been there and been so kind."

"Oh, think nothing of it. Maybe someone'll do the same for me one day, when I'm on shanks's pony. I just hope you'll find your sister weel. I'll say good night, sir."

"Good night," said Oliver. "And thank you again." And, as the tail-light of the van disappeared around the curve of the drive he took Jody's hand in his and said, "Come along now. We've no more time to lose."

Out on the road, with the headlights probing the racing darkness and every turn and curve a familiar one, he said to Jody, "Now tell me."

"Well. Caroline was sick again, and then she said she had a pain, and she's all pale and sweaty and I didn't know . . . the telephone . . . and then . . ."

"No. From the beginning. From the letter Caroline wrote. The one she left on my desk."

"She told me we were going back to London. But I said she'd *promised* to wait till Friday, that Angus would maybe be back on Friday."

126

"That's today."

"That's what I said. Just wait until today. And she said that it was better for everybody if we went back to London and she wrote you that letter, but then at the last moment she . . . gave in. And she said we'd go to the Strathcorrie Hotel just for one night, just last night, and then today we would have to drive back to London. So I said all right, and we went to Strathcorrie and Mrs Henderson gave us rooms and everything was all right until breakfast, because she felt awful and said she couldn't possibly drive. So she stayed in bed, and then she tried to eat lunch, but she said she was going to be sick, and she was, and then this awful pain started."

"Why didn't you tell Mrs Henderson?"

"I didn't know what to do. I kept thinking maybe Angus would get back and everything would be all right. But he didn't come and Caroline just got worse. And then I had to go and have supper by myself because she said she didn't want any, and when I went upstairs she was all sweaty and she looked as though she was asleep but she wasn't and I thought she was going to die . . ."

His voice was becoming hysterical. Oliver said levelly, "You could have phoned me. You could have looked up the telephone number."

"I'm frightened of telephones," said Jody and it was some measure of his distress that he would admit to this. "I can never hear what people are saying and I always put my finger into the wrong hole."

"So what did you do?"

"I ran downstairs and I saw that kind man coming out of the bar and he said he was going home and went outside, and I went after him and told him my sister was sick and told him about you and said would he take me to Cairney."

"And I wasn't there?"

"No. And the kind man got out of his car and rang bells and things and then I thought of Mrs Cooper. So he took me round to her house and she gave me a huge hug when she saw me and she told me you were at Rossie Hill. And Mr Cooper said he would take me, though he was in his braces and slippers, but the kind man said no, he would, he knew the way. So he did. And I came. And I'm sorry about spoiling the party."

"That didn't matter," said Oliver.

By now Jody had stopped crying. He sat forward on the edge of his seat as though his very attitude would make them go faster. He said at last, "I don't know what I would have done if you hadn't been there."

"But I was. I am here." He put out his left arm and pulled Jody close. "You did very well. You did everything right."

The road poured away. Up and over the hill they went. The lights of Strathcorrie twinkled far below, tucked into the folds of the dark, quiet mountains. *We're coming,* he told Caroline. *We're coming, Jody and I.*

"Oliver."

"Yes."

"What do you think is wrong with Caroline?"

"At a rough layman's guess," said Oliver, "I would say that she has an appendix that needs to be removed."

His diagnosis proved perfectly accurate. Within ten minutes the Strathcorrie doctor, hastily summoned by Mrs Henderson, arrived, confirmed the appendicitis, gave Caroline a shot to ease the pain, and went downstairs again to call the local Cottage Hospital and ring for an ambulance. Jody, with what might have been a rare display of tact in one so young, went with him. But Oliver stayed with Caroline, sitting on the edge of the bed, and holding one of her hands in both of his.

She said, already sounding faintly dopy, "I didn't know where Jody had gone. I didn't know he'd come to find you."

"You could have knocked me over with a feather when he suddenly appeared. I had you both safe and sound and back in London."

"We didn't go. At the last moment I know I couldn't go. Not when I'd promised Jody."

"Just as well you didn't. An appendix blowing up halfway down the Motorway wouldn't have been much of a joke."

"No, it wouldn't, would it?" She smiled. "I suppose that's what's been wrong all this time, feeling so sick, I mean. I never thought of an appendix." She said, as though the idea had just occurred to her, "I'm meant to be getting married on Tuesday."

"That's one appointment you won't be able to keep."

"Did Liz tell you?"

129

"Yes."

"I should have told you. I don't know why I didn't." She amended this to, "I didn't know why I didn't."

"But you know now?"

She said, hopelessly, "Yes."

Oliver said, "Caroline, before you say anything more, I think you should know that when you do get married, I don't want it to be to anybody but me."

"But aren't you going to marry Liz?"

"No."

She considered this, her face grave. "Everything's such a muddle, isn't it? I always make such a muddle of everything. Even getting engaged to Hugh seems to be part of the muddle."

"I wouldn't know, Caroline. I don't know Hugh."

"He's nice. You'd like him. He's always around, and organized and very kind and I've always been so fond of him. He's Diana's younger brother. Did Liz tell you that? He met us off the plane when we got back from Aphros, and took charge of everything, and somehow he seems to have been taking charge ever since. And of course Diana encouraged the idea of our getting married. It appealed to her sense of order, having me marry her brother. It kept everything all neat and tidy in the family. But still I'd never have said I'd marry him except for that miserable business with Drennan Colefield. But when Drennan walked out on me I felt as though I would never properly fall in love again, and so it didn't matter whether I truly loved Hugh or not." She frowned. "Does that make sense?" she asked him, muzzy and confused.

"Perfect sense."

"Then what am I going to do?"

"Do you love Hugh?"

"In a way, but not that way."

"Then it's no problem. If he's a nice guy, and he has to be or you'd never have said you'd marry him, then it would be very wrong to saddle him, for the rest of his life, with a half-hearted wife. In any case, you won't be able to marry him on Tuesday. You'll be far too busy sitting up in bed, eating grapes and smelling flowers and reading large, glossy magazines."

"We'll have to tell Diana."

"I'll do that. As soon as they've taken you off in the Black Maria, I'll call her."

"You're going to have an awful lot of explaining to do."

"That's what I'm best at."

She moved her hand, lacing her fingers into his. She said, contentedly, "We only met just in time, didn't we?"

There was a sudden, unaccountable lump in Oliver's throat. He leaned over and kissed her. "Yes," he said, gruffly. "We ran it pretty close. But we made it."

By the time they had seen her off, accompanied by the ambulance men and a plump and kindly nurse, he felt as though he had already lived through a lifetime of days. He watched the tail-light of the ambulance away, down the empty street and under the little stone archway, and so out of sight, and he breathed a silent prayer. At his side, Jody put a hand into his.

"She'll be all right, won't she, Oliver?"

"Of course she will."

They went back into the hotel, two men with much accomplished.

"What do we do now?" asked Jody.

"You know as well as I do."

"Ring Diana."

"Right."

He bought Jody a Coca-Cola, installed the boy at a table just outside the telephone booth, incarcerated himself in its stuffy interior, and put the call through to London. Twenty minutes later, with long, involved and exhausting explanations over, he opened the door and called Jody in and handed him the receiver.

"Your stepmother wants to talk to you."

Jody said, in a whisper, "Is she angry?"

"No. But she wants to say hallo."

Jody, gingerly, put the dreaded instrument to his ear. "Hallo? Hallo, Diana." Slowly a smile spread over his face. "Yes, I'm fine . . ."

Leaving him, Oliver went to order himself the largest whisky and soda the hotel could muster. By the time it arrived Jody had said goodbye to Diana and rung off. He emerged, beaming, from the booth. "She isn't a bit cross and she's flying up to Edinburgh tomorrow."

"I know."

"And she says I'm to stay with you until then."

"Is that all right?"

"All right? It's fantastic." He saw the long glass in Oliver's hand. "I'm suddenly feeling terribly thirsty. Do you think I could have another Coke?"

"Of course you can. Go and ask the barman."

He had imagined that they had reached the end of the road. That there was nothing more to be done, that the day could not possibly turn up any more surprises. But he was wrong. For, as Jody went in search of his drink, there came the sound of a car driving up the street and stopping outside the hotel. Doors opened and were slammed shut; there was a blur of voices, footsteps, and the next moment the half-glassed doors from the street flew open, and in came a small grey-haired lady, very chic in a pink-and-white suit, like icing sugar, and shiny crocodile shoes. She was immediately followed by a young man, hung about with tartan covered suitcases, bumping his way through the swinging door, because he hadn't a free hand with which to hold it open. He was tall and fair, his hair worn long, his face strangely slavonic, with high, bumpy cheekbones and a wide curving mouth. He wore pale blue corduroy trousers and a large shaggy coat, and as Oliver watched he carried the suitcases over to the reception desk, dumped them on to the floor and reached out a hand to ring the bell.

But he never rang it. For just then Jody came back from the bar. It was like a film, stopping in its tracks. Their eyes met and they were both still, quite motionless, staring at each other. And then, with a click and a whirr, the film moved again. The young man shouted "Jody!" at the top of his considerable voice, and before anyone could say another word, Jody had catapulted himself across the hall and into his brother's arms.

That night, they all went back to Cairney. The next afternoon Oliver left the brothers together, and drove, on his own, to Edinburgh, to meet Diana Carpenter off the London plane. He stood in the glass-walled arrivals lounge at Turnhouse Airport, watching the passengers come down the gangways, and as soon as she appeared, knew that it was she. Tall, slender, dressed in a loose tweed overcoat, with a little tie of mink at her neck. As she came across the tarmac, he moved forward so that he would be there to greet her. He saw the frown between her eyebrows, the anxious expression. She came through the glass doors and he said, "Diana."

She had blonde hair wound up in a thick knot at the back of her head and very blue eyes. She at once looked relieved, some of the anxiety went out of her face.

"You're Oliver Cairney." They shook hands, and then, for some unknown but obviously good reason, he kissed her.

She said, "Caroline?"

"I saw her this morning. She's all right. She's going to be fine."

He had told her everything last night on the telephone, but now, roaring northwards over the Forth Bridge, he told her about Angus.

"He arrived last night, just when he said he was going to. With this American woman he's been chauffeuring around the Highlands. He walked into the hotel and Jody saw him and there was a tremendous reunion."

"It's marvellous that they even recognized each other. They haven't seen each other for years."

"Jody's very fond of Angus."

Diana said, in a small voice, "I realize that now."

"But you hadn't before?" He was careful not to sound reproachful.

She said, "It's difficult . . . it was difficult, being a stepmother. You can't be a mother and yet you have to try to be more than just a friend. And they weren't like other children. They'd virtually brought themselves up, running wild, barefoot, entirely free. And while their father was alive, it worked, but it was different after he died."

"I can understand."

"I wonder if you can. It was like being on a razor's edge, not wanting to suppress their natural instincts and yet feeling that I had to give them some sort of a sound basis for living their separate lives. Caroline was always so vulnerable. That's why I tried to talk her out of going to Drama School and trying to get a job in the theatre. I was so afraid she would get discouraged, and disappointed, and hurt. And then, when all my fears were realized, it was so marvellous when she started to be fond of Hugh, and I thought that, with Hugh to look after her, she wouldn't ever have to be hurt again. Perhaps I did . . . manipulate it a little, but I do promise you it was only with the best intentions in the world."

"Did you tell Hugh, what I told you last night on the telephone?"

"Yes. I got out the car and went round to his flat, because I hadn't the heart to tell him on the telephone."

"How did he take it?"

"You never know, with Hugh. But I got the idea, in a funny way, he'd been expecting something like this to happen. Not that he said anything. He's a very self-sufficient sort of person, very civilized. The fact that Caroline's in hospital takes some of the sting out of having to postpone the wedding, and by the time the engagement is formally broken off, people will have got used to the idea."

"I hope so."

Diana's voice changed. "And after I'd seen Hugh, I went round and saw Caleb, the stupid old goat. Of all the irresponsible things to do, lending the children his car like that. It's a wonder it got as far as Bedfordshire without blowing up. And never saying a word to me. I really could have strangled him."

"He did it with the best motives in the world."

"He could at least have made sure the car was serviced first."

"He's obviously very fond of Jody and Caroline."

"Yes, he was fond of them all. Their father, and Jody, and Caroline, and Angus. You know, I wanted Angus to stay with us after his father died, but he didn't want my sort of a life, or any of the things I could offer him. And he was nineteen and I would never have thought of trying to stop him going off on that mad excursion to India. I just hoped that eventually he'd get it all out of his system and then he'd come back to us and start living a normal life. But he didn't. I expect Caroline told you. He never did."

"He told me," said Oliver. "Last night. We talked until the small hours of the morning. And I told him what Jody wanted him to do . . . come back to London and make a home for Jody. And Angus told me what he wants to do. He's been offered a job with a yacht chartering firm in the Mediterranean. He's going back to Aphros."

"Does Jody know this?"

"I didn't tell him. I wanted to discuss it with you first."

"What is there to discuss?"

"This," said Oliver and told her, and click, click went the pieces, dove-tailed, fitting together as cleanly as if they had been planned. "I'm going to marry Caroline. Just as soon as she's better I'm going to marry her. My job's in London, and I already have a flat there where we can live. And, if you and your husband will agree to it, Jody too. There's plenty of room for the three of us."

It took some time for this to sink in. Then Diana said, "You mean, *not* take him to Canada with us?"

"He likes his school, he likes living in London, he likes being with his sister. He doesn't want to go to Canada."

Diana shook her head. "I wonder why I never guessed."

"Perhaps because he didn't want you to know. He didn't want to hurt your feelings."

"I . . . I shall miss him dreadfully."

"But you'll let him stay?"

"Is that what you really want?"

"I think it's what we all want."

She laughed. "Hugh wouldn't have done that. He wasn't prepared to take Jody on."

"I am," said Oliver. "If you'll let me. I only had one brother and I miss him very much. If I'm going to have another, I'd like it to be Jody."

They came up the avenue at Cairney and Angus and Jody were waiting for them, sitting on the front-door step, a patient reception committee of two. Almost before the car had stopped, Diana was out of it, scrambling, not dignified at all, stooping to gather the excited Jody into her arms, and then, over his bright head, looking up into Angus's face. His expression was wary, but unresentful. They had never seen eye to eye but he had grown beyond her, and now, whatever he chose to do could be none of her concern and for this she was very grateful.

She smiled and straightened, and went into his huge, bear-like embrace. "Oh, Angus," she said, "you impossible creature. How wonderful to see you again."

All Diana wanted was to see Caroline, so Oliver unloaded her luggage, handed Angus the car keys and told him to take her.

"But I want to go too," said Jody.

"No. We're staying here."

"But why? I want to see Caroline."

"Later."

They watched the car drive away. Jody said again, "Why didn't you let me go?"

"Because it's nice for them to be together. They haven't seen each other for a long time. Besides, I want to talk to you. I've got a whole lot of things I want to tell you."

"Nice things?"

"I think so." He put his hand around the back of Jody's neck and turned him gently, and they went indoors. "The best."